Seven
Steeples

BOOKS BY SARA BAUME

Spill Simmer Falter Wither

A Line Made by Walking

Handiwork

Seven Steeples

Seven Steeples

Sara Baume

MARINER BOOKS

Boston   New York

SEVEN STEEPLES. Copyright © 2022 by Sara Baume. All rights reserved.
No part of this book may be used or reproduced in any manner
whatsoever without written permission except in the case of brief quotations
embodied in critical articles and reviews. For information, address
HarperCollins Publishers, 195 Broadway, New York, NY 10007.

HarperCollins books may be purchased for educational, business,
or sales promotional use. For information, please email the
Special Markets Department at SPsales@harpercollins.com.

Published in Ireland and the UK in 2022 by Tramp Press.

FIRST US EDITION

Designed by Greta D. Sibley

Library of Congress Cataloging-in-Publication Data has been applied for.

ISBN 978-0-358-62923-8

22 23 24 25 26 LSC 10 9 8 7 6 5 4 3 2 1

For Mark

So they lived.

—Leo Tolstoy, *The Death of Ivan Ilyich*

The mountain was full of miniature eyes. There were the yellow discs of long-eared owls, the purblind blots of pygmy shrews, the immobile domes of bluebottles, the glinting black gems of brown rats.

The mountain was full of miniature eyes, of pheasants, foxes, lizards, larks, rabbits, warblers, weevils, mink, mice, lice. And each eye was focused solely on its surrounding patch of ground or gorse or rock or air. Each perceived the pattern, shade and proportion of its patch differently. Each shifted and assimilated at the pace of one patch at a time. The mountain alone looked up, down and around,

             seeing everything at once,   keeping watch.

The mountain was a colossal, cyclopean eye that never shut, even when it was sleeping.

It kept watch on the sky, sea and land, and every ornament and obstruction—the moon and clouds; the trawlers, yachts and gannetries; the rooftops, roads and chimney-pots; the turbines, telegraph poles and steeples.

The mountain alone could see through bracken, brick, wood, cement and steel—through to the trampolines and septic tanks; the IKEA coffee tables and home cinema systems; the family-size casks of laundry gel and multipacks of buttered popcorn. The mountain alone monitored every jostle, flap and fall; every trembling clothes peg and traversing jeep; every stray cat and cow-pat.

It witnessed the arrival of Bell and Sigh, on a clear noon in January—two bright specks against the green and green-brown and brown and brown-green and grey.

It saw them park in the driveway of a lichen-encrusted house on a lower rise beneath. It saw that they drove a red van filled with dogs and boxes. It saw that they were made of wool

and boots

and hair.

Once the dogs had been set loose and the van emptied, Bell and Sigh paused to appraise the view.

Although it surpassed the full spread of its surrounds, the high, rocky land was not strictly the right shape to be called a mountain. From sea level, it appeared mountain-like, but the house itself had been built on a sharp hill above the scabrous shoreline. From the perspective of the driveway where they stood, the facing outcrop appeared to be more of a ridge or bluff—blunt but tall, inhospitable.

Gently and unspectacularly it ascended from the Atlantic, as if it had accumulated its stature over centuries. As if, over centuries, it had steadily flattened itself upwards.

It was the shape of a prehistoric bank,
a drove of smoke,   an obliterating wave,

a mud and rock and foliage barrier,

impeding,   protecting.

In the overstuffed glove compartment of the van, there was a ragged
dictionary. It had been gagged by masking tape then strangled with a gigantic elastic band. It was missing a wad of pages from the close of N to
the opening of P. A pair of compact binoculars kept it company, along
with a half-roll of toilet paper, three plastic spoons, six CDs that had
become estranged from their cases, and a poorly folded road map.

The ragged dictionary was not helpful.

Hill, *noun,* 1. A natural elevation of the earth's surface, smaller than
a mountain.

Mountain, *noun,* 1. A natural elevation of the earth's surface, greater
than a hill.

Bell and Sigh had first met at the foot of a low, pointy mountain forty
miles of motorway beyond Dublin city's outer limits. It was summer
and they were among friends they had known separately for years, and
friends of friends they had each known for only just a day—the day they
all together climbed the low, pointy mountain.

Sigh had chain-smoked his way to the summit, and never once lost
his puff, and Bell had been impressed by this.

Bell had talked her way to the summit, and never once lost her puff,
and Sigh had been impressed by this.

They had both lived in the city then, divided by scores of streets
and hundreds of sterile cherry trees; by a foul river and a declining population of house sparrows. He worked in the packaging section of a

television factory, spraying the screens with anti-static before they were wrapped. He wore an elasticised face mask that cut into the cartilage of his ears and a pair of foam earplugs that failed to fully muffle the heavy puffing of hydraulics and the communal radio at full blast, its mewl of feel-good songs. She waited tables in a restaurant where the customers regularly asked for things that didn't appear on the menu and never fully finished the food on their plates. When she lay awake at night, she could still hear the sound of china being scraped and picture lettuce leaves fluttering down the waste chute, the track marks of tomato sauce and coleslaw dressing.

A year before they first met, they had each been passengers on double-decker buses travelling in opposite directions that bumped wing mirrors on a lane in the city centre. She was upstairs in an aisle seat on the right. He was downstairs standing by the luggage rack. As the buses passed and the mirrors cracked, Bell and Sigh were oblivious. They had no reason to suspect that in the future they would know each other.

They had no reason to suspect   that theirs would be
                         a single future.

On the day they moved in together, it was the winter that followed the summer they met. As they stood on the driveway to look at the view, the idea occurred to them in unison that they might one day—a day of clement weather—climb the outcrop they looked over and that overlooked them, which was   definitely
                              greater than a hill,
                                        but smaller
                         than a mountain.

They moved in a single van-load.

They started by dismantling the dog cage and together laying it down across the floor of the boot. Then Sigh took charge of the logistics of slotting the even-shaped boxes into the crooks of irreducible furniture. He plugged the gaps created by the gnarled, bowed and serpentine jumble with pliant black sacks, unbagged duvets, cushions and towels, leaving the bare minimum of negative space.

The van body rode low on the van tyres. As it climbed the last and steepest hill, the negative space was squeezed and shifted. The load pressed hard against the back doors, threatening to burst the lock and make an avalanche of their belongings.

Their new home was a whole house, whereas the homes they moved from had each been only a room.

Their whole house was unfurnished, and so the furnishings they owned that had once been too many, suddenly, together, became too few.

The house was not new to the mountain.

It had sat up on its subjacent elevation for seven decades—a drab, roofed box girdled by countryside.

From the west-facing front, it was stoutly rectangular, with five windows, a dark-wood door and a garden path, a garden gate, a concrete garden wall. Outside the wall there were two raised beds barricaded by rotted railway sleepers. Inside there was a prodigious tree. It reached out for the chimney-pots. Its fat roots forced the ground up. They broke through the unkempt lawn. Bell and Sigh decided to believe the tree was alive, even though—because it was winter, because it was bald—they had no way to be sure.

Opposite the tree there was a telegraph pole. It was also bald, but certainly dead. Its surface was blank but for the thumbprints of old knots. It held up a cable between their roof and the next nearest telegraph pole across the field, down by the road.

Onto the east-facing back of the house a kitchen extension had been added in the nineteen-eighties, ruining its charming symmetry. Across the purple gravel from the kitchen door, there was a shed of weathered timber planks with its windows boarded up. On the edge of the field—umbilically connected to the kitchen by buried pipes—there was a tin-roofed cow barn that sheltered the oil tank.

For seven decades, the mountain had watched as new tenants moved in and out again, leaving behind the props and shrapnel of their passing. There was a laundry pole, a breeze block, a tyre swing, a partially rotted timber pallet. There was the orphaned fixture of an old satellite dish, and a marginally newer satellite dish.

The house had always remained unpainted—raw plaster grey except for the sea-facing gable, which was smattered with mustard-coloured lichen—an abstract mural painted by

fungal hyphae,   airborne nitrates,

and time.

They had chosen to move in the earliest week of January, to set themselves in step with the new year.

On their journey south from Dublin, in the shop of a motorway service station, Bell had bought a bunch of unopened daffodils. In the new kitchen, she filled an old soy-sauce bottle with water and slotted the shiny stalks through its glass mouth and placed it at the pinnacle of the appliances.

On the top of the free-standing fridge, a beacon of talismanic buds.

By then they had known each other only against the backdrop of other people—friends at first, but later, mostly strangers. In pubs, parks and buses, Georgian houses rented room by room, other people had al-

ways been a few stools, benches or seats away—above a ceiling, below
an expanse of floorboards, through a wall, behind a curtain, a pane, a
door.

It had been in public spaces,
                                    against the backdrop of strangers
that they had first started to talk about the possibility of living in a place
                                            where other people didn't.

Bell and Sigh had both been born in the middle of large families in the
middle of a decade in which large families were going out of fashion.
The overcrowded houses they were raised in had always been sand-
wiched in between other people's identical houses; the open spaces
available to them had always been periodically mowed, the trees in
rows. Neither had experienced any unusual unhappiness in early life,
any notable trauma. Instead they had each in their separate large families been persistently, though not unkindly, overlooked, and this had
planted in Bell and in Sigh the amorphous idea that the only appropriate trajectory of a life was to leave as little trace as possible and in-
crementally disappear.

This idea was the second thing they found they had in common, as
well as the above-average lung capacity.

Gradually they had lost touch with the friends of friends they'd met
on the day they climbed the low, pointy mountain, as well as the ones
they'd had for years—the ones who would have advised, had advice been

sought, that Bell and Sigh should not move in together—because they were each too solitary, with a spike of misanthropy.

But Bell and Sigh were curious to see what would happen when two solitary misanthropes tried to live together.

A refuge, a cult, a church of two; this was their experiment.

They carried from the van into the house, sometimes alone and sometimes between them: a chest of drawers with every handle missing, two frail timber what-nots, three wheelie office chairs and four mug-scarred tables. A tiny TV set, a handheld blender, two radios, six lamps, nine fruit bowls, thirteen densely embellished rugs.

Every one of the household goods they owned had been donated by family members Bell and Sigh intended to lose touch with. Somehow they had ended up with two juicers but no toaster, three dustpans but no brush, two steam irons but no ironing board, ten towels but not a single set of curtains.

As if in consonance with these coincidences, tenants past had relinquished to the officially unfurnished house: four mattresses but no bed, a block but only a single kitchen knife, a stainless-steel sink strainer, a lopsided fridge, a toilet brush, a dining table and a three-seated sofa with curlicue Latin calligraphy incorporated into the blemished upholstery.

Ubi amor . . . the sofa read, *ibi dolor.*

Because Latin, Bell said, is the language of sofas.

Then she draped the best blanket across it, silencing the twisted script with turquoise arabesques.

. . .

They had made the decision to lose touch with the families given to them by chance, and to inaugurate a new one of their own—spare but select, without regress to obligations of

gift gifting,   attendance at group events,

or love.

For the whole afternoon and evening of the day they arrived, and late into the night, Bell and Sigh studiously commingled their separate belongings. Eventually they chose a bedroom: the worst of the upstairs ones.

Upstairs, because altitude is essential to good sleep.

The worst, because they would mostly be unconscious while they were in it.

Then they appointed the best of the second-hand mattresses, pressing their knuckles into the springs, kneading the dimpled foam and debating what might be lost along with the bed frame; whether springs, slats, legs or small, swivelling wheels made some quietly significant difference to the quality of sleep.

Probably bed frames, Sigh said, are just something bed-makers want you to think you need.

On their first morning, the sky over the mountain was a lather of pink. The pinkened puddles pulsated; the briars dripped. There was a streamer of black sack that had escaped the previous day's unpacking, somersaulted down the driveway and tangled itself around the spiky branches of a scruffy spruce tree. On their first morning, it fluttered madly in the wind, as if a black flag had been raised for them.

. . .

Inside the house, tenants past had left behind their stains, wounds and signatures.

In the worst room, where Bell and Sigh had chosen to sleep, there was a wide bronzed penumbra at the meeting point of the ceiling and the gable wall. There was a fat smudge on the back of the beige door, the combined palm-marks of several years' worth of slamming. There were old cotton buds, safety pins, paper clips and colouring pencils in the splits between floorboards. There was hair of all colours—

white, gold and copper;

dog, cat and human;

brown, brown and brown.

During the earliest days, Bell and Sigh were solicitous to one another and, at the same time, shy of their keenness, their solicitudes.

Though she rarely ate white bread, still Bell would remember to crack two pieces off the sliced loaf in the freezer every morning and lay them out on the chopping board to defrost for Sigh's lunch. Though he rarely wore necklaces, still Sigh would take up the snarled ball of Bell's jewellery from the bowl in the bathroom and strew them out across the pitted timber surface of the kitchen table.

He would sit and pluck at the strings and beads and pendants.

He would tease out the knotted cord of her earphones.

Their skill sets, in the beginning, were dissimilar.

She was unable to work cigarette lighters or whistle. He was unable to change duvet covers or answer to recorded voices on the phone.

Their perceptions of certain colours differed too. They would often argue over purple, and the nebulous zone where yellow becomes green.

. . .

To their select family,   they had each contributed   a dog.

Pip, a lurcher, was hulking and dull-witted.

Voss, a terrier, was spry and devious.

Both had arrived as strays and originated from separate but comparably tragic pasts—the details of which would remain always mysterious to Bell and to Sigh. Before moving house, they had devoted lengthy discussions to the matter of how Pip and Voss might react to the change in circumstances. They were both fascinated by their dogs' fidelity to routine—their apparent contentment with the daily repetition of a sequence of mundane rituals—and by the idea that each dog lived in a state of doubt, constantly anticipating the worst.

Voss liked the new house. He liked its old smells. He liked to methodically lick patches of its surfaces where potent substances had been spilled in eras past. He liked how the upstairs windowsills began at floor level, as if they had been designed especially for him. The view was of the fields and road, the animals, tractors and jeeps that went by. It extended across three rooms and could be chased from sill

to sill

to sill.

Where Voss habitually met the world with enthusiasm and aggression, Pip was diffident and evasive. If the living room door had been left ajar, she would linger in the hallway, her cavernous eyes peering through the gap to the unreachable room, whereas Voss would shove every door with his black snout, whether it was ajar or not.

Pip also found the timber-imitation lino that floored the lower storey of the new house terrifyingly slippery. She would repeatedly hurry back to the sanctuary of the carpet on the stairs, the only porous strip

of ground throughout the whole house. She was coarse-coated and
lean, with a scooping chest and long, snaky legs. The precariousness
of her anatomy was much of the reason for her insecurity. Downstairs,
whenever she stopped to think, whenever she glanced at the floor, she
would promptly lose her footing and fall over.

    We need to put down rugs, Sigh said.

    She'll adjust, Bell said.

    Finally they compromised by designing a stepping-stone arrange-
ment of carpeting, and Pip adjusted by hopping

      from rug-island   to rug-island

              without ever touching down on the lino.

Voss would think with his right paw, raising it a few inches from the
ground to dangle mid-air,   trembling,

    as if pressing down, lightly, upon the rising thought.

There were belongings Bell and Sigh had chosen not to bring and, during the earliest days, regretted having abandoned. They regretted a
portable barbeque grill that had been corroded beyond recognition,
a camera stand that had lost a vital screw, a temperamental bathroom scale. Former housemates claimed them; unscrupulous landlords
pitched them into nearby skips.

They did not sleep well, on the mattress on the floor.

    Their sleeping positions had already evolved in relation to springs
and slats and swivelling wheels. They heaped two of the surplus mattresses onto the original, but it made no difference. Sigh was six foot;

his back often ached. Bell was shorter but had poor circulation. The chill of the floorboards seeped into her sluggish blood. Then there was the dearth of altitude. A hill and a single storey were not enough, as it turned out. An extra few feet of frame was necessary for comfort, a rectangle of negative space between boards and vertebrae.

He would stretch and curl, crane and buckle his overlong limbs. She would monitor the cold of the night—manipulating the knob on the radiator, tilting the top part of the window at various angles of openness. She would fill a hot-water bottle and slide it around between the different districts of the bed—

the level of her belly, his belly,   her feet, his feet,

and ultimately, with a splosh, to the floor.

Sigh received, after three and a half weeks, a message from an old friend, a man who was selling the house where he had lived for thirty years and had heard Sigh was in need of furniture. Providing they arranged for it to be taken away, his message said, they could have his spare double bed for free, as well as anything else that caught their eye and that he knew for sure he would not be able to keep.

They debated what they should bring as a token of thanks. Sigh suggested a card with a pair of fifty-euro notes folded inside. Bell counter-suggested a bottle of decent wine.

Because they couldn't agree, they ended up empty-handed.

On a wet Sunday afternoon, again they detached the cage from the back of the van and drove east, in the direction of the city, with Pip, Voss and Bell squashed into the passenger seat, obstructing the handbrake and the gear stick, causing the glass to mist faster than the demister could keep up with. They found the old friend's house to be at roughly the same stage of incompleteness as their own, but while his was in the process of being taken apart, theirs was in the process of being put together.

He made them coffee. They roamed from room to room, rifling through the memorabilia of a full family life—the books, trinkets, pictures, textiles and utensils of three childhoods and three emigrations, a happy marriage, an unhappy marriage, and then a divorce. Each thing was in its own way generic and vaguely familiar to Bell and to Sigh, yet at the same time unconnected to any special incident or memory from their personal histories. They could not help but feel, as they roamed, in spite of the man's kindness, desperately awkward.

It would be impolite, Bell whispered, not to single out a few things to take. It would be rude to shun every last one of his shunned belongings, and yet they were also afraid of choosing something that the man secretly longed to keep.

They found themselves most attracted to the items that were versions of things they already owned. Finally they agreed on four objects that seemed to bear the appearance of unwantedness: the frame of a double bed, a worn armchair, a dented DVD player and a teapot with a porcelain gnome sitting upright on the lid, the point of his porcelain cap bent,   drooping.

They were glad to return, in the evening, to the put-togetherness.

Sigh bought a BEWARE OF DOG sign and fixed it, with a stapler and four cable ties, to the bars of the galvanised gate at the furthest end of the overgrown lane that led up to the house.

The BEWARE warning was spelled out in red alongside the silhouette of a sitting dog. With a black felt-tip, in an attempt to make it look more like Voss, Sigh thickened the silhouette's neck, blunted the nose, crossed out the tail.

They desired additional, more threatening signs, but did not have the courage to install them.

Bell bought a huge tin of Afternoon Tea Biscuits and a pair of lunchboxes. First she made a new label for the tin, bearing both their full names in capital letters: ISABEL & SIMON. She covered it with a plastic sheet and taped it into position on the lid. Then, at the kitchen worktop, she unloaded the tin, layer by layer, and deliberated over the division of biscuits.

He would be shortbreads, jellies and wafers. She would be fingers, wheels and plains.

He would be milk, and she would be dark.

In the morning, Sigh carried the tin to the mouth of the driveway and placed it down with a rock inside.

The farmer who was their closest neighbour and either owned or rented every surrounding field had a hairless head, an ageless face. It seemed as likely to Bell and to Sigh that he was forty as sixty.

It's a windy spot you have there, he told them. This was on the first afternoon they encountered his jeep as they walked the road, the first time they had occasion to stop. On a blind corner, the farmer yanked up his handbrake, stepped down from the driver's seat and leant against the bull bars, forearms folded, engine idling, as if daring a coming vehicle to rear-end him, or as if so well-versed in his own road's schedule of traffic that he knew no vehicle—at that time, to that place—would come. At that time, in that place, Bell and Sigh didn't pay any more attention to the farmer's remark about the wind than to his other remarks—that the season was unusually mild, that he might soon be putting his cows out to grass, that he would always be willing should they ever need help.

Up until that point, they had not considered their spot to be exceptionally windswept, but partly due to a swing from lenient northerlies to prevailing southwesterlies, and partly due to the power of suggestion, in the final days of their first month, they started to notice the way the cliff funnelled gusts up from the open sea and over the fields, levelling the short grass. Opposite the kitchen extension, there was a rocky verge that the gusts bounced against, creating a river of wind that wrapped the whole way around the house.

Standing on the mountain-facing side, they noticed how the electricity lines seemed to be held in a permanent flinch, and how every scruffy spruce the whole length of the road inclined its crown away from the sea and toward the north-east, toward the mountain, as if locked in a discreet nod of respect.

The sound the mountain made was the sound of the wind moving over and through it—scudding across its rigid faces, ruffling its bristly hair.

Sometimes the mountain excited the wind

and other times   it stopped it.

Gradually it became apparent that the worst of the upstairs rooms was also the one that bore the brunt of the prevailing winds. Gales pounded the sea-facing gable. The windowpanes shivered in their ill-fitting frames. A loose gutter rattled with just enough inconsistency to be discomposing—to keep Bell and Sigh awake at night, alert and listening. Down on the gravel there was a hose-pipe that jabbed an upturned basin, a severed cable that languidly slapped the wall. There were other skittering objects they had never managed to identify; objects that were animated by the dark and vanished as soon as dawn broke.

By then they were too settled to consider a change of bedroom. Their second-hand bed had been taken apart in the garden, carried piece by piece up the stairs and crudely reassembled. Every hanger in the wardrobe had been dressed in their clothes, every shoe lined up beneath the radiator. Every scarf had been slung over the curtain rail and every cardigan heaped on the back of a chair in order of size, each hugging the smaller one beneath.

Bell discovered, bound up beneath the overgrown lawn, a blue rope clothes-line. She wrenched it free, brushed the torn grass off, and Sigh strung it between the tree's thickest branch and a bolt sunk in the side of the house. Without knowing it, they had fashioned a wind instrument. There was the flapping of wet fabric, the dull jangle of the wooden pegs, the ping of weathered springs as they came apart, the thud of timber pincers against sod.

The tree was an instrument too. The tips of its branches rapped the plaster skin of the house like drumsticks.

The house was an orchestra—of pipes and whistles, of cymbals and chimes, of missing keys and broken reeds. All January the elements played its planes and lax panes, its slates and flutes. Sometimes its music was a kind of keening and, other times, a spontaneous round of applause.

On wild days the loose gutter became a maraca.

Even on quiet days, once every three hours, the house would crack— a noise like a muffled shot   or a soft clap.

. . .

By the end of their first month, Bell and Sigh had started to notice how the undersides of soaring gannets against the sea-grey sky were astonishingly white—whiter than the gulls; whiter than the spume. They noticed how the pointed ends of the ditch-twigs had become barred by frost and, higher up, how globs of garish fungus—the sheen and shape of wax-wrapped cheeses—sprouted around the moist joints. They noticed how the flag of black sack had been blown on and ensnared anew by some nearby barbed wire.

There would be so much more.

And they would see it as soon as   practically nothing

had continued to happen

for a slightly longer time.

All January the gorse across the house-facing side of the mountain remained sinuous and winter-stripped, like a mass of upside-down lightning strikes driven into the rock. New green started to show only in the opening days of February. Between the new green, lights came out; yellow dots disarranged by the wind such that, in the full brightness of day, the gorse appeared to be twinkling.

There was still no sign of growth from the tree in the garden.

Ceremoniously, Bell and Sigh went outside and approached the trunk with the kitchen knife, and scraped back a shard of bark.

They found the flesh was clammy and green; that under the surface, the tree was still feeding,   feeling.

They found they had been right to presume it was alive.

They returned indoors, to the kettle and screens and stove, satisfied, leaving behind them,

in the moss-slicked skin of the living tree,

the green slit of
an
opened
eye.

Chapter One

The mountain remained, unclimbed,
for the first year that they lived there.

The obstacle was threefold. They were not climbers or cragsmen or even hikers. They were dog walkers, at best.

There was no obvious access from the level of the fields, no paths or lanes, no tracks visibly channelling its surface.

And Bell and Sigh had liked the way they walked on the very first evening—following the slender, battered road downslope in the direction of open water, catching sight of the sea as the ground rose and fell. There was an unhurried emerald stream, a thick central strip of lustre-less grass and barely any traffic. It ended in a beach that was pebbly at high tide and sandy at low tide, with a substratum of sea peat and an erratic population of oystercatchers.

They had liked this walk on the very first evening.

They had continued to walk it every evening since.

. . .

In the mornings, Bell alone took the dogs out along the same road but in the opposite direction, skirting the base of the mountain for approximately half a mile—to a blue gallon drum that she had designated as her turning-around spot—and home again. Sigh, roused by the sound of the kitchen door as it thumped behind her, got up and dressed. He prepared a pot of coffee, rolled a cigarette and sat on the doorstep, so long as it wasn't raining. He watched for his whole small family to return.

He was pleased by the sight of the three of them reappearing—rounding the nearest corner,

coming gradually closer,

growing larger and clearer—

their parts reconstituting, their colours restoring, and Bell was pleased by the sight of Sigh on the doorstep, waiting—his unmistakable outline, tall and stooped, back-lit by the porch-lamp, cup in hand, and on windless mornings, from in between the fingers of his right hand, an ascending curl of smoke.

She was always the first to wave.

Indoors,   during the course of their inaugural year, six light bulbs had died. Five bathroom-dwelling objects had plummeted down the toilet—two loo rolls, a powder brush, a compact mirror and a comb. Bell or Sigh had retrieved all five. Except for the loo rolls, each had been rinsed, dried,   and placed back

in its precarious spot.

Other un-flushable materials had been flushed—loose threads, a clothes label, a hair tie, a bead.

. . .

Outdoors,   the lid of their biscuit-tin letterbox had rusted. The
letters of their names had faded. The cover of the chimney-pot had
been knocked off. The chimney cover was the size and tarnished shade
of a second-hand dinner-plate, scratched white, slightly cupped.

It sailed down into the facing field and lay between the grass stalks
like a crash-landed flying saucer.

By then Bell and Sigh had lost interest in the activity of being reunited
with their possessions. Unmarked boxes with their top flaps still taped
shut had been relegated to the most-avoided corners of their least-used
rooms. Neither of them, in an entire year, had suffered the absence of
what these boxes contained, and so they ignored them.

Bell continued to reorder those possessions they had remembered
packing and wanted to be reunited with. She reshuffled the sequence
of the sofa cushions, or removed a picture frame from a windowsill to
hang on a nail planted into a wall. She transferred a pottery cockerel
from the living room mantelpiece to the kitchen shelf, or the jewellery
bowl from the bathroom to the bedroom, or a scarf from the curtain
rail to the banister.

Though she had never articulated it, Bell believed that eventually
everything would be in its right place and life would be complete,

and Sigh subliminally shared this belief,

though he never bothered to reorganise the furniture.

In the first month of their second year, a new calendar had arrived with
a man in a small oil tanker.

He dragged a fat hose into the tin-roofed barn, and stood back with the cows and watched as the hose convulsed. He left a calendar behind on the kitchen worktop, as well as a china mug, a blue biro and an extravagant invoice, each bearing the fuel company's insignia.

The calendar Bell and Sigh arrived with had displayed a different bird for every month—a mistle thrush, a turnstone, a buff-breasted sandpiper and so on—until all twelve were twisted up and consigned to the bin of recyclables. The fuel company calendar popped out into a self-supporting cardboard triangle. It was fronted by a thick pad of notelets. Each blared a date and a single line of text—an aphorism, a prophecy, a joke.

During the preparation of dinner, Bell ripped a day off and read its fortune aloud to Sigh.

Time is to stop everything happening at once, she read.

Delay is preferable to error.

Obstacles are simply stepping-stones.

By then Pip and Voss had forgotten their individual existences. Because neither of them were able to recognise their own reflection, they recognised each other instead, and presumed that this was what they looked like. After only a year, Pip saw herself as a ragged terrier and Voss wholeheartedly believed he was a handsome lurcher.

Voss stretched out to nap across the best of the duvets they kept on the floor. He woke to snap at Pip whenever she barked abruptly at nothing or startled him by forcibly sneezing. He finished his own food fast enough to finish her food if Bell or Sigh wasn't watching, and yet because Voss was fierce and violent whereas Pip was gentle and placid, it was she who was granted the freedom of not having to wear a lead as they walked.

The fields belonged to Pip, the gorse thickets and glades, the swamps. She soon developed a problematic habit of running away in pursuit of rabbits.

The clever rabbits understood that stillness was the simplest form of subterfuge. The stupid rabbits took off. On the undersides of their tails, white handkerchiefs of surrender had been pinned in order to betray them.

Bell and Sigh were furious with Pip when she ran away, but only at first, at the stage at which she was running and they were shouting her name and being ignored. By the time she ambled up the driveway, hours after the official walk had ended—panting and pausing to try to cough up the tuft of kit rabbit clogged in her windpipe; her legs coated with mud, her chin dipped in blood, her ears and tail slackened by remorse—they were only ever relieved.

They discussed the matter of Pip's precarious right to freedom.
Sigh thought she should be shackled, for her own good.
Bell thought she should remain unshackled, for her own good.

It was still the beginning,
        even though they felt as if a lot of time had passed.
In the beginning, Bell took charge of the worry.
She worried about carbon-monoxide poisoning and black ice on the road. She worried about an electrical power surge striking when the kettle happened to be empty, or a cinder falling though the shutter

of the log stove when a polyester glove happened to be drying beneath. She worried about a minuscule UFO that had entered Sigh's left eye in the midsummer of their first year and never re-emerged.

Sometimes he could feel it lodged beneath the lower lid. Other times he was certain it was tunnelling upwards, following the light, struggling to deliver itself.

Bell worried

about their internal organs generally and skin cancer of the scalp specifically; about a lump in Sigh's neck that was only a gland and a lump in her knee that was only a bone; about how she appeared to piss too often and Sigh appeared not to piss often enough. She worried that the fluctuating pattern of their pissing was not psychosomatic, as she had convinced herself it was, and that as a consequence of her constantly dismissing it as such, a real and serious problem was being neglected.

Bell worried about failing to sufficiently worry.

At this point Sigh intervened to take charge of the worry, and Bell delegated herself responsibility for the daily slippage of domestic surfaces instead. These were mostly made of fabric. There was the bedspread that rucked and the rugs that wrinkled. There were the towels that slithered from their hooks and the turquoise throw blanket that was tugged gently downward for three hours every evening by the combined force of their

sitting, squirming, slumping   on the Latin sofa,
          to pool around the soles of their feet.
It was Bell who smoothed, straightened, re-hooked and un-pooled; who hoisted

every slipped surface

back up again.

They argued—in their second year as they had in their first—over the
season in which February fell.

Sigh, on the side of winter. Bell, on the side of spring.

Weather systems arrived from the Atlantic and raced across their
valley of sky. There was a vacillating rainbow, a paroxysm of wind, a
spasmodic shower of hail. And then, the next day, there was an unbro-
ken traffic jam of low-slung cloud backed up between the sea and the
mountain, ironing the panorama away, moulting fine rain.

The fine rain greased the surface of their road, at first. Later the
tarmac became engulfed in places by puddles that stretched from ditch
to ditch, clean through the grass strip, roughly the length of a man
prostrated. The next day the puddles were gone. Each left behind the
outline of its recession in the sediment. Each recession reordered the
black confetti of gravel.

He sneezed like the piston of a steam train. She sneezed like a laser
beam. They argued whenever they thought they had sighted an unusual bird. Sigh dismissed it as the misconception of a common species,
whereas Bell always claimed that it was rare.

On calm mornings, the silt fully settled. The man-length, road-wide
puddles mirrored the sky. On frosty mornings, a wafer of ice obscured
the mirrors, and Bell out on her morning walk could inspect the ghostly

tendrils of grass roots, the fragments of half-buried, bleached-out litter, and how they moved as if   adrift   in space.

On the wettest and windiest days, they stayed inside. They switched off the radio and listened to the house in full voice—to the rustle and drip, the whistle and howl. Sometimes these were comforting sounds, and other times they were   pernicious.

Even when they stayed inside, the weather reached them.

The kitchen extractor fan spat misdirected specks of rain and the log stove blew puffs of smoke into the living room. Even though the bedroom window was double-glazed and shut tight, still the scarves Bell kept draped over the curtain rail billowed, as if the house had a weather system unique to itself.

On the low hill, weather commanded their days.

It conducted activities,   dominated conversations,
                    occupied thoughts.

Along with the tyre swing, the laundry pole and its buried line, the pallet and satellite dishes, two bins had been left behind by tenants past. One was for compost. It stood against the garden wall, anchored to the spot. The other was a wheelie bin three-quarters full with sodden ash. Its axles were seized. Its contents had set into cement.

One was faded green and the other was faded black, but on dull days they seemed to be the same colour, and on days when the wind was easterly and strong, their lids blew open and held in the air and quivered, as if shyly waving to each other.

Ever since their first meal in the new house, Bell and Sigh had collected every substance they supposed to be compostable in a plastic bowl on the kitchen countertop. Every time it reached capacity, they conveyed the bowl to the bin, tipped its contents across the surface of a matter almost as cement-like as the ash, though lumpier and less purely grey.

And there it sat, scattered, refusing to mix.

We need to stir it, Bell said.

Sigh fetched the kitchen broom. He turned it upside down and ploughed circles through the jumble of inhospitable substances. The onion skins got caught up with the outer leaves of Brussels sprouts. The tissues enshrouded the apple cores. The coffee grounds coated the carrot-stubs and fell inside the broken eggs and the shells of pistachio nuts, the soft husks of hollowed-out kiwi fruits.

They made no attempt to use the ash bin.

Instead, they slowly filled a tin bucket that was kept on the tiled dais beside the log stove. On wild but dry days, Sigh stood at the top of the driveway and shook out the bucket, and the wind snatched the ash and shaped it into a blizzard, and the blizzard diffused and its particles spread out so swiftly and widely and sparsely that they never settled.

Crows breathed them in,

                         dew dissolved them.

Bell and Sigh monitored the growth of daylight, impatiently. By February they would be sick to death of the confinement of winter—the flint sky, their stagnant rooms. There was the sticky dust, the shedded fur and old smoke. There was the morning-after stench of last night's dinner: fish fried and garlic roasted, the tomato paste that spat onto the hobs and burned.

Underneath the tree, beside the compost bin, the mud-lid of the raised vegetable bed was punctured by hardy weeds: hairy bittercress, groundsel, scutch. On a fine day, Sigh trowelled out the weeds and stirred the cleared earth with the butt of the broom. He hosed it down and laid a rectangle of blue tarp in an attempt to summon earthworms.

Then he built a fence of timber posts and chicken wire. He fashioned a second garden gate from the partially rotted pallet. At ponderous pace, it took three days to enclose the part of the lawn that was not walled. The idea was to better keep the dogs contained, but on the third day, with the erection of the final post, Bell tossed a ball that accidentally bounced into the facing field and Voss made a running jump, vaulted off the patch of lawn under the tree where its roots lifted up the earth,

and cleared the wall with equine grace.

Pinned to the noticeboard in the kitchen, there were two bin collection schedules, one for the year they were in and one for the year gone. Each was the size of an elongated postcard. Bell had drawn circles around their dates of significance: Sigh's birthday, her birthday, the birthdays they had invented for Pip and for Voss, and the anniversary of their inaugural encounter, and of their arrival at the house.

During the first year, they had developed a habit of narrating the dogs, of putting words to their grunts and whines and woofs, providing a voice-over for their probable thoughts.

Voss had a deep, husky voice like a mafioso. He was most likely to be self-declaring. Pip had a high, soft voice like Scarlett O'Hara. She was most likely to apologise.

. . .

The small strand to which they walked on the first day was neither long nor sandy enough to have been officially named. They had come to refer to it as 'the beach', as if it was actually beach-like,

as if it was   the   only   beach.

The oystercatchers broke apart and retreated each new time they arrived. Every evening the alarmist seabirds were startled afresh.

They lingered on a large bench-shaped rock above the tide line, keeping watch on a prominent reef out in the cove that perpetuated a ceaselessly cresting wave. There was a grey seal that reared its head to check on Bell and Sigh. From under the surface of the water, the seal was able to smell the business of the shore. The scent of humans was stronger than dead crabs,

stronger than raw slurry,

stronger than the millions of molecules of rotted seaweed freckling the shallows. They played seal bingo, trying to be the first to spot the next place where he would pop his head up.

From a short distance, the freckles disappeared. From the point of view of the mountain, the breakers were unrealistically white.

From the point of view of the mountain, the breakers were

bog cotton,   cuttlebone,   snow.

Every evening as they walked, Bell and Sigh described to each other the weather, scenery and character of their route, of the given evening.

In a field, an old tin bath had been substituted for a cattle trough, still with its seized and rusted taps attached. In front of a peach-painted bungalow, there were two stone eagles, an ornamental cabbage in a Grecian urn. At a sharp bend in the road, there was a telegraph pole encircled by a clump of creeping ivy so dense that it resembled a tall, hairy figure standing, fidgeting in the breeze. There were rodents in the ditches that darted away as they approached, songbirds that flew up like flares, and tens of thousands of gangling fuchsia branches, creaking out hushed conversations.

Every evening as they walked, Bell and Sigh remarked to each other how strange it was to believe that the hedges had ever been laid by men. They described the small changes since their last walk, a full day ago. A crisp piece of litter—unburied, unbleached—a fresh clump of silage, an unfamiliar pat of shit, a snowdrop, a stonechat, a shattered snail.

Every evening as they walked, Bell and Sigh

repeated themselves,

extravagantly.

A cattle path ran parallel to the human road that skirted the base of the mountain—a track of rubble and pebble the farmer had gouged through his bumpy fields.

Opposite the end of the driveway, halfway up the hedge that masked the cattle path, there was a patch of conspicuous paleness. Sigh was convinced it was a gap. Bell thought it was more likely a fluctuation in the even tone of the vegetation, a flourish of lighter-green plant, a section of withered leaves. The only way to be sure was to witness the moment when a cow passed behind it.

But no cows passed.

They were all still captives of sheds and barns, their path awaiting repair. Its surface had been loosened by frost; the lime of its stones liquefied by rain.

Hovering high above the paleness in the hedge, there was a spot of brilliant white on the rock of the mountainside. At first they thought it was a sheep that never moved. Then they thought it was a sheep that had died but never decomposed,

a sheep whose corpse had turned
            to marble.

Bell and Sigh compared dog bites, healing and healed.

It was always Voss who bit them. He panicked sometimes, and bared his teeth, and flailed his bared teeth about in a defensive frenzy, aiming at whatever happened to be closest, hurting those he had intended to keep from harm.

They exchanged news of other small cuts and their progress into scars. Together they traced back to the origins of a bruise.

They exchanged news, in the mornings, of their respective sleep.

Their bed was a sea.

Their bed was all the seas together, mussed and moiling—the untouched Arctic patch north of their necks beneath the pillows, the straits around their twitching feet, the truncated expanse of Mediterranean in between them, its melodramatic warmth.

Because they had to share the pale blue sheets and floating blankets and body heat, they were each reflexively responsive to the other's agitations.

They either
both slept poorly   or both slept well.

On still nights—a sniff, a sigh, a shallow snore, a sip and swallow, the swishing of unselfconscious limbs.

When they slept well, they dreamed, and never remembered.

When they slept poorly and remembered a dream, they attempted to retrace its origins, as if it was a bruise.

I dreamed, Sigh said, that I pulled a baguette from a holster.

. . .

They wanted to be the kind of people who woke early, naturally. Instead, most mornings they slept through three snooze cycles. They had trialled every different tone: glissando, quantum bell, popcorn, scampering. It made no difference. They tipped their warm, unwilling limbs out from beneath the duvet onto the cold floor. They reconstructed the previous day's clothing.

In February every surface of the house was as cold as the cold floor—the walls and worktops, the knobs and banisters. They each wore many layers—of nylon, blended cotton, canvas and wool. When they went outside to walk, they would take off rather than put on.

Sigh, out of a sense of duty to Bell's superfluous worry, bought a carbon-monoxide detector for the bedroom—a rigid oval of cream-coloured plastic. It was supposed to be positioned around the height of a person's chest; at the altitude of the lungs into which the poisonous gas would be inhaled were it present, but there was only a bedside locker and a chair, so Sigh stood it on top of the wardrobe.

Higher than every other object in the room, every thirty seconds the detector emitted a pinhead green beam. During the day, the beam was barely visible, but in the dark its flash was like the lamp of a doll-sized lighthouse drowsily spinning on its axis,

a slow-blink   across   the night sea.

In the garden centre, Sigh bought a sack of peat moss to feed to his raised bed, and Bell bought a trolley-load of the kind of potted plants she believed might be hardy enough to withstand her habitual yet unmalicious neglect: succulents, cacti, geraniums, spider ivies.

Back in the house, she decked the surfaces of their ramshackle furnishings with the resilient plants. She chose the most damaged of the bowls and placed them beneath the perforated pots in the assumption that she would remember to tend these new, green members of their small family; that she would remember so often and feed them so earnestly that the excess water would flow clean through their saturated soil, and well up in the chipped bowls.

Sigh re-stirred the compost bin. He lifted the blue tarp off the raised bed and sprinkled the peat moss and re-stirred the mud.

There were new weeds then, but no sign of worms.

Bell stocked the principal fruit bowl with mangos, avocados, satsumas and limes, two unsteady storeys high. She placed it on the living room windowsill, where it created a bumpy, rolling horizon; where it overlooked the sea across which the fruit had sailed to reach Bell's bowl. In the far distance, there was the silhouette of a cargo-ship stacked with fruit-coloured monumental containers.

They succeeded in eating the mangos and satsumas. The limes were used up slice by slice in tumblers with tonic and gin, but the avocados had been so unripe to begin with that by the time they finally ripened,   Bell had forgotten them.

There was always so much to be thought about,

to be decided upon.

After she had shaved every black bit away, there was almost nothing left.

The facing field remained empty through every February except for the ungrowing grass and, occasionally, a fox that Voss always spotted first.

Voss maintained a near-constant watch from one of the three upstairs windows. Every time he saw an orange slash of fur crossing the
empty field, he would raise the alarm by frantically yapping.

Fuckit! The FOX! It's the FOX FOX FOX! Fuck off, FOX! FOX
FOX FOX, fuck-itty-fuck-fox-off! Bell shouted to the tune of his
barking.

GOOD BOY! Sigh shouted, when the dog finally stopped. We
would all surely have perished were it not for you.

They had come to know Voss's alarm calls; to differentiate between
them. For farm machinery lumbering along the road, he issued an un-
certain   woof,   pause,   repeat. For the wisp of
a smell through the open window, an invisible mink or foolhardy cat,
he grumbled gently. For the clattering approach of the farmer's jeep, he
broke into explosive snarling and flailed his bared teeth,

  attacking Pip,

        attacking the duvet,

        attacking the door saddle.

The only person who ever rang the doorbell was the lady who came bi-
monthly to read the electricity meter. Whenever Bell and Sigh noticed
the approach of her little white van, they would hide—lying with the
flat of their bellies against the rag-rugs or pressed to the scuffed walls
like frightened reptiles.

Couriers soon knew to sound their horns, drop the package onto
the welcome mat, and drive away.

Downslope at sea level, with the onset of March, flowers came prickling
up—new flowers, even though each March it felt like a form of return.

The stubbly yellow grass started to bush and green again. Pink-streaked daisies were the first to nose through the dirt lawn, between the gnawed sticks and dismembered pegs, the skinned orbs of split tennis balls. Narcissi with their sherbet scent soon followed, dandelions shaking out their manes.

In the opening days of their second March, there was a creeping warmth, a spell of rainlessness. Bell picked a medley of lawn flowers and brought them inside to the soy-sauce vase. Still it sat on top of the fridge; by then it was ringed with brown grime.

Hares and pheasants started to cross the facing field along the path channelled by the fox. Rabbits became so numerous that Pip could no longer be bothered to chase them. Finally, cows were restored.

A herd of young bullocks,   brawny, skittish.

They were strangely princely beasts—no showing ribs, no trace of ringworm. They had velveteen ears and huge, twinkling eyes and as many chambers in their stomachs as in their hearts. They trundled over to the flying saucer. It had sat in the same spot in the field for over a year. They bent down and tasted it with their elephantine tongues.

From one or other of the upstairs windows, Voss maintained surveillance on the bullocks' daily movements. He watched over their group circumnavigations and individual circumvolutions, their gathering together and breaking apart, their adagios and allegros and protracted intervals of open-eyed slumber. Beyond his line of sight, a herd of cows paraded along their repaired road to the parlour every dawn, and back to the fields shortly after, and over again every dusk from fields to parlour, from parlour to fields.

The whirr of the milking equipment filtered over the hill with first light,   as if this was the sound of first light, the anthem of the day coming.

In the aftermath of night rain, the tune would be accompanied by sloshing. If the night rain had been heavy, the cows would appear strangely puffed, as if they had been hosed down by showers, blow-dried by gales.

In the aftermath of mist, they developed cow-drips.

At the lowest point of each belly, a distended teardrop.

The farmer kept a stump-legged horse. It stayed out all winter wearing a waterproof poncho, with buckles and straps.

A pair of donkeys materialised over a wall along the route of their evening walk. Both were classically patterned—brown with a dark cross over the withers. Neither wore a poncho. Instead their coats were ashen, caked with mud. Their teeth were blunt and every hoof curled upward like a jester's shoe.

In the deep pockets of her raincoat, Bell carried the floppiest of the carrots to the donkey field and chucked them, strategically, over the low stone wall. She was cautious of moving too close or too fast and startling the donkeys. She was mindful of aiming the carrots in order that both would be apportioned their share.

In the beginning, there was a handful of things that Bell and Sigh disagreed upon—the designation of the doors of the house, the speed at which time passed, the necessity of dental hygiene products—Sigh, on the side of mouthwash, Bell, on the side of floss.

Bell considered the front door to be the one opening out from the kitchen and on to the rock-facing side of the house, the shed and the place where the van was parked—because this was the door they used the most. Sigh considered the front door to be the one opening out from the hall and on to the field-facing side of the house, the garden path and gate and the garden—because this was the door they used the least. To Bell, front meant at the forefront of daily use. To Sigh, front meant to be positioned centrally, on the main side of the house.

There was only a single key for each of the exterior doors. One for the back, one for the front; whichever was back, whichever was front. They intended to have a spare set cut, but had not yet got around to it.

Each day on the hill passed in parcels of time that had evolved without being allotted: the morning-walk parcel, the morning-after-the-morning-walk parcel, the lunch parcel, the post-lunch-and-pre-walk parcel, the post-walk-and-pre-dinner parcel,

                                 the night.

Though Bell and Sigh spent the whole day within calling-out distance of each other—together arriving at every new hour; together retreating from every old hour—still they argued over the speed at which some parcels seemed to have passed.

Bell was often resentful that Sigh perceived a few hours to have barrelled when for her they had straggled. She was better at inventing activities for herself, whereas he had superior patience.

She was quicker to anger, whereas he had a cavernous, agonising capacity for regret.

A robin had claimed ownership of the fuchsia hedge that ran half the length of the east side of the driveway.

It scaled the apical branch each dawn, and no matter the severity of the wind, it gripped on with its claws and trilled a melodious warning song—a beautiful, convoluted ballad about the murderous vengeance that would be exacted upon any bird who dared to trespass.

The robin of the driveway had murdered in the past.

It was prepared for murder.

They forgot the earthworms.

The blue tarp sagged.

Rain, crow shit and ash collected in its shallow cavities, form-ing a thin gruel that Sigh spilled onto the lawn one bright evening. He peeled the tarp back. She carried two cushions from the sofa outside to the cleanest stretch of salvaged railway sleeper. One bright evening they perched there beside the weeds, flanked by the dogs, encircled by the useless fence, sipping from mugs of whiskey that had been heated up, watered down and laced with honey. A half-moon of clove-stud-ded lemon floated in each. They were facing past the windowless gable, down the driveway, across the human road, a field and the cow road, to the mountain. They were each holding its stare when they remembered in unison that a whole year had passed

and they had not climbed it.

It was inarguably spring, again, the green of fern fast supplanting the grey of rock, and they were still looking in the mountain's direction when a cow passed behind the patch of conspicuous paleness in the hedge that masked the cow road, and together they saw how Sigh was right—it had never been a plume of light plant or a section of deadness, but was indeed a gap—

an empty space,   an oval of nothingness,

an opened eye.

Chapter Two

The mountain remained, unclimbed,
for the first two years that they lived there.

It remained unclimbed as the oil tank emptied and was refilled.

It remained unclimbed as the rain smeared away Sigh's modifications to the BEWARE sign; as the neck and nose of the dog were slimmed down again; as the tail reappeared.

It remained unclimbed as the bunches of leeks and beets Bell bought in the farmers' market doffed their mud and small slugs into the drawer at the bottom of the fridge;

as the mud accumulated,

and the slugs subsisted.

It remained unclimbed as a groove in the soft, pummelled surface of the mahogany table beneath the front-facing living room window overflowed with the residue of Bell and Sigh's daily activities: wheat germ and pencil shavings, linseed and dandruff.

It remained unclimbed as cobwebs built up in every corner of every ceiling of every room, and became weighted down with dust and split apart. Then the dusty fronds of old webs garlanded every nook, wafting on a breeze so light that nothing else in the house showed any sign of feeling it—not the tassels of the throw blanket, not the daintiest leaves of the spider ivies.

It remained unclimbed as the batteries inside the carbon-monoxide detector ran flat, and then the smoke alarm—
as the latter ceased to blink, and the former commenced to chirp,
once every sixty seconds,   out in the dark hall—
like a supermarket checkout,   or an orphaned chick.

Late in the March of their third year on the low hill, a cold mouse abandoned its draughty crevice in the garden wall and made a running jump for the kitchen door. Sigh was around the corner tending to the bins. He didn't see it streak across the lino and squeeze itself beneath the skirting board in an act of miraculous compression. Neither Bell nor Sigh knew it was there until four nights later, when they were woken by an intermittent scratting, a purposeful nibbling.

The mouse had chosen the hot press cupboard—its musty warmth, the choking stench of insulation foam—as a good place to settle and craft a nest from the unpicked strands and unspun fibres of a wool jumper that belonged to Bell and had shrunk in the wash. The mouse worked hard through its fourth, fifth and sixth nights, refusing to be discouraged by groggy human voices and the flicker of electric lights, by the occasional earthquake of angry thumping. It paused only to creep downstairs and scour the groove in the living room table for crumbs, to lick the butter block in its unprotected dish.

. . .

The butter block sat out all night and day on the kitchen countertop, vulnerable to tendrils of broccoli, specks of uncooked couscous, bread-crumbs—and after the kitchen floor had been swept—dust and dog hairs rising,   swirling,

          fastening on   to the naked planes of fat.

Bell and Sigh discussed how best to deal with the mouse situation.

    She defended the efficacy of humane traps; he was sceptical.

    They settled it by doing nothing.

The farmer passed in his slurry spreader, with an entourage of birds.

    He started fires every spring, in the aftermath of a dry stretch, tar-getting the highest, scrubbiest, stoniest, most gorse-mangled tracts of his fields.

    By their third year, Bell and Sigh recognised the menacing fra-grance—of needles blistering, branches blackening, yellow petals pop-ping like embers—and the frowzy quality of dark the smoke created, distinct from that of an advancing downpour or of dusk. After real dark had settled, the smoke vanished and the flames formed a clear shape. For a whole strange night, the landscape burned and it seemed, to Bell and to Sigh, like a transient kind of cataclysm.

    The following morning, their view was a necropolis of smouldering limbs and soil. The corpses of those gorse-dwelling creatures that had failed to outfly or outrun the inferno lay charred and strewn, their eggs smashed and cooked. In the weeks that followed, Bell and Sigh were as-tonished by how fast the greenness revived, as if with a stamina rejuve-nated by cataclysm;

                       as if with a vendetta.

. . .

The gorse flames tongued the pedestal of the mountain
                                                    and stopped.
Even though dry gorse was plenteous across its fire-facing side, somehow the blaze knew that it   must   not   touch
                                                    the mountain.

Bell and Sigh could never bear to listen to the radio on Sunday afternoons, when the running commentary and background clamour of a
match or race or game monopolised every station. Sport was, to them,
a language of its own from which they were excluded. If, on a Sunday
afternoon, one of them left the radio to play on past lunch—past the
mass, past the news, past all analyses of the headlines—this was a sure
sign of acute despair; when the noise of a large crowd cheering changed
from a banal source of irritation to an exceptional source of comfort;
    when a loathed noise was preferable
                              to the piercing silence of the house.

On Sunday afternoons of acute despair, to escape the sport, together
they would set out in the van.
    A few miles outside the bounds of their rented property, there was
a gigantic hedgehog made from woven willow, an inlet allegedly inhab-
ited by otters, a padlocked folk museum and an old man who lived in a
broken-down bus with a tortoiseshell cat. There was a Norman castle,
a Victorian estate, a famine graveyard, a prehistoric stone circle, three
different geodesic domes.
    In March, the light yet low, the leaf buds splitting, catkins dripping,
Sigh, who was usually driving, accelerated as much as the dangerous

bends allowed, following a trail of new green, chasing blue gaps in the fracturing sky, as if on a mission to hound out the winter,

and shepherd in spring.

They played sad music as they careened and sped.

Bell, in the passenger seat, singled out a stray, scratched disc from the glove compartment and fed it into the slot, delicately, because the slot did not respond to roughness or to haste. It hesitated before accepting each disc, sucking it in as delicately as it had been offered.

By then a green pelt had grown on the black plastic backs of the van's wing mirrors. Inside the glove compartment, the thumb screw of the compact binoculars had become jammed with crumbs, the half-roll of toilet paper had been reduced to a few loose sheets, and one of the three spoons had gone missing. Sweet wrappers and cigarette butts rattled inside crushed coffee-cups. A handful of bone-shaped dog biscuits slid to and fro on the dashboard.

Inside the green-pelted black plastic back of the right wing mirror, a garden spider had sewn a beautiful trap. During every journey, it took refuge behind the adjustable glass. After every journey, it mended the damage done to its tenuous web by the force of rushing air and whipping briars.

It mustered up fresh silk; it darned each new hole.

A different, less industrious spider took up residence in the hollow bars of the steel gate. Another lived in the rubber hollows of the welcome mat. And there were dozens distributed throughout the house—

in alcoves, cupboards, ingle-nooks,

in open spaces and plain sight.

The largest house spider kept to a cranny beneath the bathroom
radiator by day. By night it crawled into the folds of the towels or slid
down the gently slanted sides of the bathtub. In the morning, Bell or
Sigh—whoever happened to discover it first—had to dangle a corner of
the bath-mat down like a rope ladder;

> like a lifebuoy.

To the spider, the tub was a snowy fjord, a glacial valley—vast, un-
marred, arresting. It knew this was an unsafe place. Still it could not
quell a desire to summit the tub's outer edge. Each time it was blinded
by a white glare,

and lost its footing,   all eight of its footings,
> and skied.

Everywhere they travelled together in the red van, there was the static
smell of sweaty raincoats, sour coffee, fishing gear, the dog-soiled duvet.
Everywhere they moved, beyond the windscreen, there was the mo-
tion-blurred countryside,   invariable, obscure.

Do you want me to talk? Bell would say when she wasn't already
talking. Bell talked blithely. She needed no response. She gestured toward the ivy-eaten roofs of ruins, the brambles that tumbled from their
glassless windows.

I'd say, she said, that would be about in our price range.

They parked up, and waded through the nettles and goose grass,
and peered into the backward-facing windows. In reality, nothing was
within their price range. They lived off social welfare payments and
dwindling savings. They had become poor and shabby without notic-
ing. Sometimes there was, fixed over the twig-filled fireplace of the
ruins they courted, a Sacred Heart of Jesus, its red glow lancing the
gloom.

. . .

They did not like to ask people for favours—the landlord, the farmer. Asking meant owing, in the long run. Better by far for the boiler to remain un-serviced; for the red van to be left with its front wheels stuck in a ditch for a day or two.

Better by far   to be cold,

                to walk;

                        than to ask for favours.

Along the scenic strip of coast downslope from Bell and Sigh's house were the lavishly renovated versions of the ruined vernacular cottages and farmhouses—their triple-glazed, open-plan, stone-clad descendants.

Monstrous and ghostly, they remained empty for ten months of the year. Model sailing ships and cylindrical glass vases cast lonely shadows on the windowsills. Deeper inside the dark rooms, in drawers, wardrobes and cupboards, belongings selected especially for holidays had been put away. Accessories of relaxation, relinquished to the un-scenic seasons. Espresso machines and bolero parasols. A bread maker, a foot massager, a full set of stainless-steel barbeque tongs.

Every March the farmer removed the poncho from his stump-legged horse. The donkeys had learned to anticipate Bell and Sigh's daily arrival. They gathered at the dip in the wall where Bell stood to target them with vegetables. Though at first it was only the wizened carrots she carried, later she went grocery shopping especially for the donkeys.

For the donkeys, Bell scrubbed and topped a miscellany of roots. She chopped up the stalks of the broccoli florets. She minced the hard cabbage hearts.

On the St. Patrick's Day of their third year, far from the parades, a buzzard crossed the sky of the donkey field and its earthbound shadow crossed the grass, superseding the buzzard,

three times its size,   a beat behind.

Bell went outside and sat in the garden. She insisted, even though it was cold and most days damp; even though the scenery was scorched and cadaverous.

There were dock leaves beneath the soles of her runners, shrivelled shit and the dogs themselves—Voss resting on Pip's wide chest to keep his hind quarters from the damp earth. There was the clicking of the electric fence, the scuttle of a licked-out yoghurt carton. There were dead squeak toys, sticks, buoys, fragments of masticated plastic. She looked up and noticed a luminous tennis ball wedged in the gutter; a yellow felt moon partially eclipsed by roof.

How Bell admired   the personalised squalor.

Upstairs, from the garden-facing window of the room where he sat, Sigh saw Bell settled on the kitchen chair she had hefted outside, in her duffel coat and a woolly scarf, and the huddled dogs.

How Sigh admired   her determination.

There were other dogs.

They spied them in the distance, traversing a field, goading a herd of cattle, loitering in the driveway of a bitch on heat. When they were out walking, Pip and Voss sniffed the absent dog's traces, following its digressions—

trailing the dog   who trailed the fox
who trailed the rabbit   who trailed a patch of sweet grass,

a grave of bulbs.

Only the Jack Russells caused a ruckus, raining down in a shower of penetrating yaps.

There were so many bits, by then, of black bag, feed sack and bale wrap flying from protrusions—the sharp corners of the farmer's tin-roofed barns, the thorny branches of the abbreviated hawthorns, the splinters of the timber fence-posts.

The posts stood like totems around the circumference of the facing field. They echoed the telegraph poles, never coming into flower or leaf. Instead, they leaned and disintegrated,

rotting from the inside out,   caving in.

All spring Bell and Sigh emptied the contents of the dustpan directly into the garden. They cut their hair and scattered the brown locks for the nest-building birds.

Two starlings gathered up the human hair and assembled a nest inside the vent of the bathroom extractor fan. They lived off larvae pecked from the cracks between the roof slates, the folds of the bark of the tree. They learned to mimic the other birds, the clicking of the electric fence, the chirp of the exhausted smoke alarm. Sometimes a whole flock came tearing through. Their call was the cry of a Catherine wheel; their congregation a display of fireworks.

On a mist-choked morning after a night of hammering showers, Bell and Sigh found the facing field full of mud-spattered herring gulls rooting in the wet sod loosened by rain and hoofs. They donned boots and fetched the shovel. She disbanded the gulls and kept watch as he sifted through the softened patch the birds had selected and extracted the worms, tugging them free like long, severed lips, dropping them into an oversized mug—until there were a dozen or so, and together Bell and Sigh condemned them to the compost bin, to drown in coffee grounds, garlic shells, dog hair.

From then on whenever the wind blew the bin lid up, she would say: the worms are trying to escape.

A blue bath-mat swung from the clothes-line.

The mat was pure cotton, non-slip. The line was not long enough to accommodate a full load of washing. They draped the excess socks over the fence and so the chicken wire, by their third spring, had started to sag.

When the winds were high and the line was overburdened, the sheets dragged the raised bed, supping the watery dirt. Bell pulled the line up again and new rain rinsed out the treble-pegged, perpetually hanging mat.

They greeted it last thing every night when they let the dogs out to piss. Pip never pissed or even crossed the threshold of the front door. She only stuck her head out into the cold and divined the night air with her twitching nose. Voss pissed, but he spent a long time selecting the right location. He circled the shadowy lawn,

doing his   security checks.

The blue bath-mat had been on the washing-line since the beginning. Even when they needed to hang out a full load, they never thought to take it down. Even when it did dry, they never brought it inside and placed it on the shelf where it should have belonged, with the folded hand towels, or draped it over the side of the tub and used it.

They had forgotten its use. The bath-mat had come to seem to be a
small section of the steadfast panorama,
                              an aperture popped out of the muddy blue.
They had forgotten whether or not it had originally been blue. It
seemed possible that it might not have popped out of the sea and sky,
but soaked them up instead.

April—wild garlic in tremendous clumps the whole length of the driveway, its scent squashed free by the tyres of the van, and the hedges
dense and high again; the plastic flags re-pinned by new growth, the
fungus smothered, the barred twigs reconditioned into points. Swallows in their red bibs arrived and clogged up a joist in the cow barn
roof with mud and straw.
    Jupiter appeared, in their third April.
    It grew brighter
    and then dimmed again.
    Lady's smock materialised in the facing field, and calves in the field
immediately beyond the facing one. The humps of their bent backs
were barely visible above the replenished hedges—brown, grey, black,
beige—like broad, smooth stepping-stones.
    The further away the cows, the more it appeared as if they were
constantly still. The closer cows moved like clock hands—orbiting
the chimney-lid; their positions shifting though their bodies never
seemed to.

Voss chased the cattle in the garden, even though the cattle were not
in the garden. Sometimes a curious bullock advanced upon the electric
fence, craning his neck toward the disarrayed, succulent lawn, and Voss

would spot him through the garden gate and skid down the concrete
path savagely yipping, halting a half-second before colliding with the
iron bars, and the bullock would clatter away, across the open expanse
of the facing field;

                 every other bullock scattering   in sympathy.
The individual items of lawn squalor moved like clock hands too,
             like the cows,   like the cosmos.
    They switched places, loomed in and out of sight. They casually
disseminated,

           shot,   exploded.

They tried to make the trip to town no more than once a week, on
Tuesdays, but often ended up making it again, on Fridays or Saturdays,
if the provision that was running low happened to be one amongst
their quadrumvirate of groceries: coffee

                                        kibble

                                        porridge

                                        whiskey.

In town, they attempted disguises.
    They had matching cotton caps bought from the fishing tackle
store—crocodile green with sickle-shaped peaks. They wore them to
partially obscure their faces, and sometimes sunglasses, if the season
was right. Only the occasional checkout assistant remembered them,
and a homeless man with the word TIM carved into his forehead, who
was in the habit of asking Sigh for money because Sigh had the kind of
face—even when partially obscured—that invited such solicitations. It
had happened to him in the city too.

. . .

April was a vacillating month. One day it was summer-like, the road-wide puddles receding, leaving behind their spectre in a brown scum. The next it was winter again, drops of cold rain clinging to the new buds, to every prong of the barbed wires.

The stinging nettles flourished, and every spring Bell and Sigh challenged each other to eat them, discussing how best to disguise their sour flavour—in soups or stews, deluged by soy sauce. They didn't fully trust that the felled spines of the cooked leaves wouldn't prickle their throats; that the acid of their stomachs would successfully subdue the bitter weeds.

Then they forgot.

Saint days, feast days and festivals came and went.

Bell and Sigh were only aware of their impending arrival or recent passing by means of the evidence left on the supermarket shelves or the faces of the people they saw in town. In spring there might be boxes of pancake batter encircled by plastic lemons, or a grey smudge of charcoal in the centre of the checkout assistant's forehead, or potted shamrock lingering amongst the bunched daffodils, pyramids of chocolate eggs flanking the bakery section, a line of chocolate rabbits queuing in parallel to the human queue,

each swaddled in gold foil,   throttled by a bow.

In the windows of the primary school, paper chickens had been pegged by their blood-red feet along a line of string.

On the lawn outside the church, a timber pallet had been painted with the words   HE

IS

RISEN

Some Tuesdays they visited one or both of the town's two charity shops—the smaller was in aid of an animal rescue, the larger was in aid of a suicide prevention service.

In two years Bell had bought from the rescue and suicide shops— and then arranged and rearranged inside the house: a pair of shell earrings, a box embedded with glass beads, a knitted hot-water bottle cover, an extendable desk lamp, four rugs, five novelty mugs, eight charmingly patterned ceramic bowls, and a rigid plastic figurine of Elrond.

Elrond was nine centimetres tall. He wore a brown gown and a crown of thorn-like matter. His right hand was beneficently extended. At first he had been positioned in the centre of the living room mantelpiece above the dais of the log stove. A shrine had since developed around him, extending across the full length of the shelf in either direction. It was composed of origami doves and periwinkle shells, wood buttons, glass pebbles and purple incense cones on miniature porcelain plates. Prayer flags and chains of carnation flowers dripped from its rim.

In the beginning, Bell had made attempts to hide her superstitious rituals from Sigh, most of which involved touching, lightly, as if in bestowal of a blessing,   or perhaps
          in an effort to draw   a trace of blessedness
          out of the touched thing   with only her fingertips.

There was the touching of the blue gallon drum that marked the turning-around point of her solo walk, and the touching of the dogs' heads before she served their daily sardines. There was the touching of the Elrond figurine whenever she passed it, and the touching of Sigh as soon as she woke in the morning—whether he was awake or not—whatever part of him she was able to first find above or beneath the duvet.

The other superstitions mostly pertained to the number of times an insignificant action needed to be replayed: the cranking of a tap, twisting of a key, stirring of a pot. Four was her cardinal number, the number of members in their select family. Bell tried always to crank and twist and stir in fours, but there were times when she had to settle for a multiple of four or,

at the very least,   an even number.

Bell was mistrustful of the odd numbers—their prickliness; their flippancy.

In the beginning, Sigh tried to hide from Bell: the noises his body made involuntarily—his belly, chest and throat—the gurgles, squishes and pops
of fluid and food,
air and smoke.

They talked
about how dog biscuits all appeared to be formed out of precisely the same matter. First the dog biscuit matter was infused with different colours. Then it was extruded and sliced into different shapes. Finally it was baked into stone,
charcoal, salmon, beige;   circle, star, bone.

. . .

They talked.

Their talk was mostly composed of the obvious, but sometimes it contained declarations and commands, or involved problem-solving, speculation, philosophy.

Their talk circled and repeated.

It added up.

It stealthily became immeasurable.

Most of their problems were solved first in speech.

There was the problem of the new rice and how many minutes it took to cook. There was the problem of the headlamps of the van and how their angle might be adjusted. There was the problem of whether or not it was sensible to trim the whole lawn with only a dull pair of shears, and of where the caustic soda, the nail clippers, the key for the shed might be, and who had used it last and what circumstances were most likely to have befallen it since.

They talked about the bits and pieces of family they had left behind, back in their autonomous lives. They wondered aloud, in intricate detail, whether or not to face down the embarrassment of having lost touch in the first place,   and get in touch again.

They settled it, as had become their habit, by doing nothing.

There were times when Bell and Sigh talked about doing a thing so much and so often that they came to believe it had already been done. In their third April, they checked the raised bed for signs of potato shoots, and only then remembered they had not planted anything, but only talked about it.

It was not too late, in their third April, to plant potatoes.

In the garden centre, they purchased two nets of Sharpe's Express seed potatoes. At home they knelt before the railway sleeper and followed the instructions printed on the net's label. They churned up the solidified mush of mud and peat moss. They buried the wrinkled lumps in shallow trenches, heaping the excavated mud into ridges. It was during this process that Bell found, deep beneath the surface of the bed, a perfect potato—brilliant pink, unblemished, unrotted.

You know if you eat the everlasting potato, Sigh said, you live forever.

But she only buried it again.

And their rows and the gaps in between their rows were wiggly, the height of the ridges uneven, and at the instant that the job was finished, they saw all the ways they could have done it better—with manure stolen from the opposite field or seaweed from the beach; with wider holes, taller ridges, straighter rows.

On the road they walked, there was a bend on a steep rise, and once every few weeks below the bend, Bell and Sigh found an object that had fallen from a trailer during its skewing ascent, or out the back of a tractor, the open boot of a car, and rolled to the gravel edges of the road. A stump of wood, a length of twine, a socket-head screw, a bicycle reflector
like a tiny, blurred moon

amongst the pennywort.

And aluminium cans—not just at the point of the steep bend but spun out along the road, in various states of decay, embedded in various strata of the undergrowth.

And mounds of horse shit, though neither Bell nor Sigh had ever witnessed the farmer's horse stray from its field. Rain broke the shit down. The diluted fibres fertilised the grassy seam. And slurry-spills—a trail of puddles the dogs paddled home with them on the pads of their paws. After a dry day, the slurry set like marmalade on the surface of the tarmac. Voss liked to lick it, sneakily.

He would drop a few paces behind, pretending to sniff.

The mountain witnessed

the stump-legged horse jump its wall to shit on the road, and every piece of hardware that fell and rolled. It witnessed the Lucozade bottles and takeaway boxes cast from car windows after dark, the gloves lost by careless, warm-handed walkers.

It witnessed murky shapes crouching in the hedges that might be pheasants and might be hubcaps and might be a rusted toaster, a discarded deep-fat-fryer. It witnessed, on the road, a broad slash of petrol—leaked, seeped, a terrestrial rainbow—and at the same moment, directly above the petrol spill   an actual rainbow appeared,

faint as a soap bubble.

Fortune favoured Voss.

A squeaky pork chop lay in the grassy seam of the road below the bend one evening, and a week later there was a cat toy with a tiny bell inside. He conveyed them home to the hearthrug. He gnawed them to bits, swallowed the bell. The hearthrug was where Voss stored his tennis balls. He rarely destroyed them completely. Instead he plucked away their tight fur with his prickly front teeth, thoughtlessly consuming slivers of disfigured plastic and tufts of luminous fuzz.

Voss was an acrobat.

Sigh did his best to retrieve the tiny bells and slot them inside cracked buoys to kick about the garden. He fastened strings around balls to swing through the air and tow in spirals. He stuffed biscuits inside old socks and tied knots in the ankles.

Bell and Sigh were acrobats then too. They had developed previously unimaginable throwing, catching and dodging skills. They had become ambidextrous.

Pip preferred soft props. She never bit or ripped but tossed and pounced. She filched socks and knickers out of Bell's laundry basket and flung them into the air of the bedroom and caught them, every time, unless they landed where she could not reach—on the bed or wardrobe, across the rim of the door.

When Pip lay down, she folded her cumbersome limbs with remarkable precision, as if she were a deckchair.

When Voss sat down, it was mostly on Pip.

By then if any one of them was alone downstairs, they were always able to tell who was moving about upstairs—

by the pressure of footsteps on floorboards,

by the weight and pace,

by the patter of claws,   or not.

After weeks of silence, the mouse who lived in the hot press began to chew on the electric cables as a means of filing down its relentlessly lengthening teeth. When the lights started to flicker, Bell and Sigh agreed to put down a humane trap. They fashioned a homemade one, guided by photographs on the internet, out of a clothes peg, a wire coat hanger and a plastic bottle.

They baited it, ironically, with a pink chocolate mouse.

It was caught on a Saturday night. The bottle tipped on the wire axis of
its see-saw structure. The mouse's claws grappled against the un-grip-
pable plastic. On Sunday morning, Sigh poured it into a poorly rinsed
milk carton and they drove out into the countryside.

The van was a cocoon of sharp smells and loud, sad, spattering
music. A big bag of dried sprat had replaced the dashboard biscuits and
every CD was gruellingly skippy.

They drove until they found a man-made woodland with a mossy,
puddled path cut through, and Sigh released the mouse by spilling her
fear-stiffened body into a glade of bluebells,

>   where she died of trauma,
>   with flakes of sour milk in her fur.

Voss slipped into a single mud-sock on their way back along the path.
On the drive home,

>   they noticed white blossom,   thick as cloud,
>   drifting and dropping like April snow.

The spider who lived in the hollow bar of the gate never built a web in
wind or rain, only when it was calm and foggy; when the chewing of the
cows was the loudest of the night sounds; when the sweep of the fox's
brush passing through the nettles was deafening, and in the morning,
when the sun could be heard rising, there was a gentle grinding.

In every hedge the gorse-dwelling spiders stretched silk between
needles and the ground-dwellers threaded strands through the road's

grassy seam. The ground webs resembled pale vortexes that whorled down into central points, into pinprick holes.

And at the core of every ground web,   there was

an entrance, an absence,

an eye.

Chapter Three

The mountain remained, unclimbed,
for the first three years that they lived there.

By then the roof had shed three slates. Each lay in shattered pieces on
the driveway like un-cemented crazy paving. Two more tennis balls had
become lodged in the moss and mulch-choked gutter. A strong gust of
wind had carried grass seed up there that sowed itself and sprouted.
Timorous stalks peered over the PVC parapet,
        and bearded the balls.

Other gusts had snatched three socks, a pair of underpants, a tea-
towel and a pillowslip from the washing-line and scooted them across
the facing field. They skimmed dock leaves and glanced off cows. They
shrank into the middle distance,   and
    finally   dissolved
           like specks of scattered ash.

The blue bath-mat, leaden with rain, had overwhelmed its storm-
proof pegs and slumped onto the lawn. The silhouette on the BEWARE
sign had faded

           to a dog ghost.

. . .

The windowsill above the kitchen sink was crammed with the light pots of dead and dying herbs. The knob for the top oven had lost its grip on the short steel rod that protruded from the dashboard of the cooker.

It slipped from each notch,
                              shunning every setting
                                        to smoothly spin.

All but one of the wine glasses had suffered chinks and been condemned to the bottle bank. A single plate and the lip of every mug was chipped, but Bell and Sigh continued to use them, until the chipped bits took on the stains of the substances they sipped—the pink, green and red of speciality teas, the dark brown of milkless coffee.

By then they had carried home from town
              a great mass of ground brown beans and dried oatlets,
              ten thousand pellets of meat-flavoured mixer and two
       thousand lumps of coal,
              a hundred apples, a hundred onions, a hundred eggs,
              a bathtub of strawberry yoghurt,
                                        a white lake of milk.

By then they had twice seen
              a magpie sitting on a cow,
       but only once
              a cow with a cable tie secured around his forehead
       as if it was a sweat-band,   or a tiara.

. . .

Many times the cows had escaped

and circled the black box of the house in the dark, like pilgrims, casting about for each other, for the way back to the field.

Sigh, who was usually the one to put the dogs out to piss last thing at night, had made a habit of sticking his head around the door and then standing on the step to clap and scare the passing fox, the pilgrim cows.

They still had not had a spare set of keys cut. By their fourth May, there was little need for separate sets; they invariably came and went together.

As invariably as they came and went together, they brought the dogs along.

In the beginning, they had left Pip and Voss behind in the house when they went grocery shopping and the back of the van would be taken up with bulging bags, except for a corner of the dog duvet that they reserved to buffer the fragile items—a box of eggs, a pot of basil, a perfectly spherical, easily bounced, easily bruised melon. Until one day it occurred to Sigh that the dogs, after they had watched as he and Bell made their preparations for leaving—lifting down the empty bags from their hook, gathering keys, phones, wallets; zipping up coats—after they had listened to the locking of the house and the slamming of the van doors and the engine as it growled to life, had no means of being sure that Bell and Sigh would ever come back again; that they had not been

casually   abandoned.

And so the passenger seat was flipped down; the dogs brought along. Bell and Sigh squashed the groceries in around their feet and cradled the soft fruits in their laps and shouted at Voss for trying to eat all his food for the week on the way home.

. . .

It was still the beginning, even though three springs had fully passed.

Three springs had taught them not to expect buds on the tree in the garden until early May, and not to expect the branches to puff up with feeble leaves until even later, sometimes as late as June.

Three springs had taught them the cycle of untended lawn flowers—from pink-tinted daisies to rangy buttercups—and every weed in its latest permutation, and how goldfinches would come for the dandelion heads—

plucking them, nervously;   swallowing even

the plumes.

There was a narrow, unkempt strip of terrain between the concrete garden wall and the field fence. It had taken Bell and Sigh three years to notice it. It was as long as the house and a half but only as wide as a doorstep. Another partially buried railway sleeper lay there, as if propping it open.

Either side of the sleeper was corralled by feathery grasses, common vetch and, in one corner, the five doleful yellow hoods of a cowslip.

Had it been there all along—the unkempt terrain—they wondered, or was it widening, the sleeper-prop extending,

softly pushing   the garden wall   off

from the field.

Sigh had been sorting pencils, one afternoon.

They came from old boxes and cases and desk organisers. They were stubby and chewed and blunt. He rose from the place where he had been sitting and approached Bell, who was sitting in a close-by but different place. He leaned over her shoulder and held them out. He splayed them across his open palm and fingered through their skinny trunks, pencil by pencil, jabbing them apart.

Him is yours, Sigh said, and him, and him,

because Bell liked the 4Bs and over, whereas Sigh liked the 3Bs and under.

She was graphite and charcoal; he was every kind of H.

The May sea warmed.

A septic algae blended with the seeped slurry and broke into bloom. It turned the tide red and saw the fish off.

Whenever the cows were on the far side of the facing field and out of sight, Sigh practiced for when the red tide passed and they would be able to fish again. He took up his rod, hopped the fence and stood fixed to the same bald spot, his pitcher's mound,

and swung around,

pivoting his hips, lunging his arms and shoulders after the shooting lead—as if in fury, surrender, supplication—and then reeling back in, pausing to pluck locks of grass and scraps of dock leaf from the weight's wire grippers, and then starting over again,

casting out.

The dock leaves reached a storey higher than the grass. They looked as if—instead of stretching up from beneath—they had each sailed down from above,   and settled.

The May sea turned blue again and mustered up a ripe crop of plankton.

Then Bell and Sigh struck out to the small strands and gentle cliffs surrounding their hill with rods, reels, rigs, pliers, bags; with Pip and

Voss rattling around amongst the raincoats and buckets in the back of the van.

The noise the line made as it unspooled at top speed several feet above the surface of the sea was distinct from the noise it made shooting over the facing field. Sod sucked in the whizzing sound, whereas salt water flicked it up and out—a whispery drumroll that ended in a startling splash.

Mostly they fished for the feckless, tasty species—mackerel, bass and pollock to fry, grill and bake—but after a spell they always grew curious about what else it might be possible to drag up from the fathomless depths.

They went to the marine atlas on the internet that plotted the contours of the seabed.

They plotted the contours of their seabeds,

and stood on the shore, drawing weed-decked beasts up to daylight—fish with square skulls and tangerine skin; fish the shape of long, fleshy capes; fish with adjustable lamps protruding from their foreheads and miniature sharks with freckles descending in size from belly to spine, with sandpaper skin and feline eyes.

They conducted an examination, and then Bell held each fresh specimen high in the air for the mountain to admire.

The sharks peeled back their gums and champed their jaws. They smacked the air with their tennis-racket tails. Bell and Sigh, after a moment, released them.

The sharks swam away, 　　　　　　　　　　unharmed.

Or they blundered in circles, bumping the rocks, gulping. They floated back to the surface against their will.

. . .

It was Bell who held them up to the mountain because it was Sigh who dragged them from the sea.

It was Sigh who had learned how to fish, back in his autonomous life, and who carried with him most acutely the memories of all the times he had caught nothing. Sigh remembered every night he had sat for hours alone on slithery rocks in drizzle and mist, every snapped line and lost lead; every tangled flotilla of weed; every beast that slipped its hook and swam away with a steel lip-ring and a gut full of stolen bait; every old boot.

Bell fished gauchely, unburdened by the past. She took greater pleasure but demonstrated inferior patience.

She wandered off with the dogs, ambling laps of the high-tide lines, dipping like a wading bird to collect the shells of yellow periwinkles, flat oysters, variegated scallops, rubber ducks and drift-sticks.

There was once a stone the perfect size and shape of a fist—a fist with each finger curled tight and its thumb stuck in the air. She kept it in the overcrowded glove compartment, and took it out and lifted it up, every now and again, to express approval.

In the evenings Bell arrayed the drift-sticks in front of the stove, criss-crossing the hearthrug in a shaky grid.

Clear dawns sliced through the curtainless bedroom window and woke Sigh. He got up and went to the edge of the field to dig for earthworms, or he drove to the estuary with a long-handled fork for mudworms—rag and lug. He ladled them up from their miry tunnels with a scoop-shaped trowel and sealed them inside a set of re-used takeaway containers.

Both sides of the ragworms' bodies were lined with legs through which they breathed. The lugworms were shorter and lighter, with hispid gills and mucus-coloured tails. Threaded onto hooks, the two species were indistinguishable—their ends pulped together; their insides reversed.

Bell was woken by Sigh's absence.

She got up and waited on the doorstep with a cup of coffee and a cigarette, with Pip and Voss, and when he returned with his worms of all kinds, they walked the morning walk together—along the path skirting the base of the mountain. Together they touched the blue gallon drum, and turned back again.

An impression of a worm in every situation, Sigh said, and closed his eyes and wriggled his shoulders and neck very gently, almost imperceptibly.

There were tunes—intros, themes, choruses. Bell and Sigh caught them individually in the ordinary course of a week—from TV ads, from tracks played on the radio. Then they infected each other—humming the same jingle, chanting the same rephrased lyric, until the tunes became

mangled,   untethered from their sources,

their lines re-worded,   their words re-formed.

Flourishes of samphire and kale appeared on the supermarket seafood counter in summer, decoratively placed to best set off the tails and scales, the twilled fillets, a rosette of whole sardines and ten salmon steaks in the configuration of a heart, studded with cherry tomatoes and sliced kumquats.

There were times when Bell and Sigh entered the supermarket with the intention of buying porridge, but—entranced by the floristry of dead fish—left with

six   small   squids   instead.

Each squid, no matter how small, had a single bone, frail as a bay leaf and bay leaf shaped yet transparent, un-tearable, un-snappable, micro-waveable—nature's plastic.

Sigh was the one to trim and tidy their seafood for Bell to cook, rinsing off nematodes and tweezering out needle-bones, extruding the squid's black beaks with his wet fingertips.

The nights grew milder and they longed
for a means of sleeping outside without the hassle of moving their second-hand bed or inventing a new bed; of having to dismantle everything again as soon as it rained. In the end they only opened the window.

Inside their night bedroom, the air was spiked by an astringent scent of slurry.

Inside their night bedroom, they would hear, and fail to hear, and think they heard: the clicking of hunting bats, the hoarse shriek of a barn owl, the night cows rattling their chains, and a slow car on its way home from the pub,

the beams of its headlamps tracking across the room
from right to left,   inch by inch illuming
the ceiling stain.

And yet still they lit the log stove with the dried-out, dismantled trellis of drift-sticks—not because they were cold but because the glow of the glass was intrinsic to the comfort and catharsis of evening, as was the clack of the locking door, the grumble of the fan oven, the prattle of the TV, even the smoke that rose from their oil-burnt frying pans. It didn't matter what they cooked nor the heat it was cooked at, the smoke rose, fogging up the kitchen windows, making their eyes glisten.

The houseplants continued to survive. The cacti bloated and dilated the rims of their pots. The succulents had babies. The spider ivies tripled in length—weeping from their shelves and sills, clawing the coats of the dogs as they passed, twining around the table legs.

Even a red geranium that stood on the top of the log stove had refused to perish. Bell or Sigh usually remembered to lift it down as they lit the stove, but every once in a while they forgot and an ugly, chemical smell filled the room as the plastic pot melted and glued itself to the porcelain dish.

The geranium seemed fine at first, but gradually its leaves tanned and crinkled, and they felt guilty, and overwatered it, and lifted it up and down, realigning its wasted pot in order that every ruined leaf met the light for a day.

Sometimes Bell filled the sink with water,
                   set the smaller pots afloat.
And the plants drank
                   until they sank.

They spent a full fine day, in the May of their fourth year,
         squatting on the grass beside the compost bin,

upending plastic pots and tipping the earth out into sandcastles, prising the plants from their compacted moulds, untangling the brittle roots. Then they installed the cuttings in fresh peat moss and new private vessels—sawn-off plastic bottles and yoghurt pots, their bases stabbed with holes. For the first time, Bell and Sigh drew up some of the mush of their own compost bin, though its stench was strange, though at the very bottom it was dotted with identifiable objects: the stone of a nectarine,

the rind of a hard cheese,   a corn cob.

Once they had finished, there were five times more houseplants than there had been in the beginning. They set them back in the old places and chose new places. It was as if their rooms had come suddenly into leaf.

To create new surfaces, Bell and Sigh conveyed three years' worth of potted herbs—their entire pot-bound herb garden—from one side of the kitchen windowsill to the other, and piled them into a salvaged trawler-box between the yard tap and the drain.

The basils and corianders had been pinched away to stubble and would never grow back. Though the parsley seemed to have died, outside it started to regenerate. New crimped leaves came free from the sprigs and spread.

The thyme fared best of all.

It was a place where thyme thrived.

On the finer evenings, they walked on past the beach and its bench-shaped stopping rock. They left the road and followed the imprint of a path that led on around a slender, precarious peninsula.

The peninsula inclined and rounded off into a hundred-foot cliff drop. At the highest point, strong winds kept the gorse short and the spare grass strangled by heather of three sorts—bell, heath and ling. Skylarks and meadow pipits nested there. The unhurried emerald stream sawed a cleft and met the open water.

In late May every cliffside hummock was clumped with kidney vetch and sea pinks; the heath scattered with spotted orchids, tormentil, speedwell, bog pimpernel, pin-leafed thyme. Bell picked a few pin-leaves, crushed them between her finger and thumb, and held them under Sigh's nose. To Sigh, the scent bore a trace of familiarity. It was similar to the potted supermarket variety and at once cleaner,

sweeter,   sharper.

On either side of the faint path, a hundred feet down,

      waves thrashed even when it was calm.

The sea there had a momentum independent of the wind. The offense of gusts aggravated only its surface. Its waves were driven by a propulsive force that ascended from the earth's crust, impervious to the atmosphere. A yellow-white coagulation became caught between the reefs after a few days of persistent roiling. Light birds of froth flew up to land and clung, quivering, to the weave of wildflowers and scrub.

There were walks when the sea seemed certainly to have increased in size. There were walks when Bell and Sigh were fully convinced that the open water was engineering a decisive yet unhurried advance   upon   the mountain.

At the edge of the surface of the peninsula, four monumental letters had been formed out of shallowly planted flat rocks. E I R E, they spelled—a message for passing aircraft from almost eight decades before. Once every couple of years, the local historical society would come and scrape back the creeping topsoil, and they had erected, as a marker, a national flag on a short steel pole that Bell and Sigh set free, one afternoon during a summer gale, and watched as it tacked across the sea—

a tricolour sail　　　　without a vessel.

The panorama from the tip of the peninsula included a rock island a mile offshore. It was no more than a knoll but lofty and jagged, marked by a beam of light in the bottom centre—a gap that the dropping sun, on cloudless days, gleamed clear through—and on the through-gleaming days, they marvelled at the visible presence of the archway, at the brilliance of the absence at the rock knoll's heart.

If it wasn't for the island, Sigh said, you wouldn't even know there was a hole.

In June the nettles they had failed to eat flowered. Inflorescences popped and lolled from the stems like midget grapes, like downy spores.

In their fourth June for the fourth time
the garden tree came into flood,
foliage mushrooming from every bud.

The mess of twisted, whiskered limbs exploded against the horizon. Its profile went from a line drawing to a watercolour, from spiked and tapping to fluffed and murmuring.

They woke to the sound of light rain even though it was not lightly

raining. What sounded like rain were the new leaves and pendant-like
flowers crashing softly against one another, and on calm days, the hum
of feeding insects. The canopy was opulently green from above but
paler beneath—the underside of every leaf was

blanched,   chalky.

Every June, the garden tree revealed itself to be

a sycamore.

Every June, Bell and Sigh remembered the full greenness of the mountain; how bright and brash this bluff so usually

barren, dull, rough.

Swallows in the cow barn roof.

Starlings in the extractor fan; trailing straw down the unpainted
plaster. They had learned to imitate the strangled chatter of the radio,
the melody of piss hitting porcelain.

Sparrows beneath the eaves, and a bat no bigger than a watch-
face—gripping on by its muscular toes, nosing out from beneath a loose
shingle—and a magpie pecking in the mulch of the gutters, in between
the bearded tennis balls,

panning for gold.

A smooth newt on the mudbank of the stream. It held eerily still as
they approached, a toy dinosaur.

In the ditches, stitchwort, silverweed and hogweed sparred for position. In the garden, a row of lilies along the west wall reached taller
than the grass, taller than the dogs, taller than the wall itself. They
were not quite lily-white, but ivory. On the washing-line, there were

bed-sheets scarred by the shit of songbirds, auras of blue inside a halo
of cream,   like burgeoning mould, like developing bruises.

And the grass bloomed and grew—chasing the lilies. Sitting cross-
legged on an outspread blanket, Bell and Sigh were hemmed in by stat-
uesque stalks. They lost sight of the small dog, of everything beyond
the brow of the wall—

    the facing field,   gone,
    the sea   gone,
    the ridge of greened mountain,   gone.

There wasn't a mower, only rusted shears on a hook in the shed, and
on a dry afternoon Sigh attacked the overlong grass with its creaking
blades. He began at the east fence on his hands and knees. He finished
at the west wall with blistered palms, a stigmata of fly bites and a dim
ache low in his back.

Across the lawn, several of Voss's lost balls lay

                            exposed, exhumed.

That fucking dog, Sigh said, he always wins.

By then their daily ceremonies were numerous and elaborate.

Many of them revolved around cleaning, though the house was
rarely ever clean, only temporarily neater. Those objects that had accumulated a conspicuous quantity of filth or shifted free of their appointed spot would be wiped down, put back.

They slung the rugs across the garden wall and used the handle of
the broom to flagellate them. With each blow, the rugs let out a puff of
dust and ash and moulted fur, a muffled cry.

They changed the light bulbs,

rarely remembering to buy new ones. Instead they robbed the
lesser-used rooms in order to keep the most-used constantly lighted.
Eventually they were forced to bulk-buy—push-ins, screw-ins, halo-
gens, incandescents—and move from ceiling to ceiling, mounting and
dismounting a chair.

They brought their emptied glass to the bottle bank,

taking it in turns to hold a vessel at the mouth of the appropriate
bin—mostly CLEAR, occasionally GREEN. They hesitated before letting
go, to relish the smashing of the preceding vessel. There wasn't any bin
for BLUE, and so the bottle of fancy gin left over from Christmas was
repurposed, every year, as a flower vase.

Most of their ceremonies revolved around dinner.

Bell cooked in a language of burnt bits, tomato bases, the inappro-
priate inclusion of parsley. She assembled each evening meal with the
colour wheel in her mind—the primary shades of staples mixed, blitzed,
coddled and braised into secondary and tertiary colours; the white
and orange flesh of potato, the purple blood of beetroot, the plumes of
obligatory kale—all within the confines of a plate.

She had come with cooking skills. He had come with the ability to
fish. He had brought his tackle. She had brought a pair of pans and a
loaf tin, a baking tray, a hand blender, an egg-whisk.

When Sigh cooked, it was in the way he believed Bell liked: red,
with green flecks, lightly burned.

They never started to eat until after one of them had remembered
to lightly touch each dog's head;

until after they had performed a toasting of forks.

. . .

Whenever they ate noodles, there was always too much.

Sigh mimed the tugging of an invisible strand from a nostril which, in turn, raised the corresponding foot.

The first potato plant was dug up in the final week of June. The stalks were thick, the leaves sprawling, and so they were surprised to find comparatively little root. The smallest spuds were the size of hazelnuts, the biggest no bigger than an egg. The crop of a single plant filled a cupped palm.

They dug up a second plant, a third. They ate the whole patch—two months of supervision and anticipation—in just six sittings.

They used the largest, lightest bowl to pick their own potatoes. It was the same bowl they used for everything. It helped to soak the labels off spice jars and facilitated the mixing of myriad doughs and the mashing of innumerable potatoes. By then the bowl had cradled tens of frozen king prawns as they daintily melted. It had held

seashells,   nut shells,   pasta shells.
It had caught vomit.

Voss liked to keep constantly mindlessly busy. He did regular rounds of the kitchen floor, snuffling, snorting, his head hung low, and then the perimeter of the sofa and every other site where Bell or Sigh might have eaten anything at any stage of the day. He played kill games with tennis balls, ballcocks, buoys, sticks, bones and stubby kelp stems. Bell collected them from the beach and Sigh posed as puppet master; conjuring the inanimate, insentient props to life, pretending to care as much as the dog did.

Voss was scrupulous in the execution of his pointless activities; he was passionate. Only the peas that rolled under the sofa escaped the sweep of his lengthy tongue.

Then he would retire to sit on Pip.

Pip was more inclined to kill time by sleeping.

Bell and Sigh found the first tick embedded in her scooping chest, poking out from an infected lump as she slept stretched in front of the fire.

At first Bell tried to get the tick drunk by dripping whiskey in the general direction of its engorged mouthparts. Then Sigh tried to make it dizzy by spinning its jutting end in counterclockwise circles with the pad of his index finger. Eventually he ran out of patience and wrenched it free with the tweezers they used for boning fish. The tick's abdomen tore away from its dorsal shield and its head broke off inside the dog's body.

Bell placed the abdomen, like a jewel, into a plastic tub that had contained liquorice allsorts and still had dots of sugar

sticking to the base, skittering into place

like pink and blue punctuation marks around the butchered arachnid. The next day they all together paid a visit to the vet.

The vet examined the dog and confirmed she had an infected bite.

The vet examined the tick and confirmed it had no head.

Then she replaced the tick in the allsorts tub and handed it back to Bell, and Bell carried it home and deposited it on the top of the fridge where the junk mail, coppers and elastic bands lived—items that were

not quite rubbish, and not quite useful. There was an old phone char-
ger, a packet of sundry Band-Aids with only the useless circular sort
left,
　　　　　　　　　　an inflatable travel pillow,　　　　　　　deflated.

From the first tick on, they frisked the dogs often for swollen bumps,
the protruding nubs of blood-sucking parasites. They tore the head off
every time, and kept the bodies in plastic bottles, jam jars, light bulb
boxes. They piled them into a tower on the top of the fridge.
　From the first tick on, Bell and Sigh wore drainpipe jeans all
summer long, ankle-boots and knee-socks.

They did impressions of the little dog preparing to shit. He tended to
shuffle, part-crouched, sniffing for precisely the right spot, approaching different hummocks of grass from different angles, testing different
positions.
　He took his time, oblivious to their teasing.

They saw porpoises out to sea off the tip of the peninsula.
　And followed the fins as they breached, beating a land-bound parallel until the land ran out and the fins became shags or guillemots,
shadows or ripples.
　They heard lizards beneath the surface of the measly cliff grass. The
sound they made was swifter than a vole, sharper than a shrew. Bell and
Sigh never saw the lizards, but on their way home up the low hill, between fields again, every twisted branch would appear to them like
　　　　　　　　　　a reptile's grappling paw.

. . .

A successful trip out was one in which they met no one.

But the prolonged evenings lured people from their electrically lighted rooms. On the beach, on the cliff path, on their road, strangers appeared—in walking shoes and high-visibility vests, with silicone drinking bottles and fashionable dogs, with a callous disregard for the fact that the beach, the cliff path, the road—and every view, every porpoise pod, peeping seal and crash-diving gannet,

every newt—belonged to Bell and to Sigh.

At first they switched the hour of their walk from the last before dinner to the last before dark.

Then, one night, they brought along headlamps and a hacksaw. They waited until after dark and discreetly decapitated the signpost that the tourist board had erected at the mouth of the peninsula. They drove home and hid it behind the bait freezer in the shed. Later on they moved it to the gap beneath the Latin sofa, amongst the rolled peas.

There was too much real light, some Junes.

Late walks left a glut of hours in the middle of the day.

They spread the blanket beneath the lilies and splayed there listening—with the dogs—to the suspicious perambulations of the bullocks, the threatening threshing of a low gull's wings, the hostile advance of a tractor.

They stood at the gate for hours passing the binoculars between them, watching an unusual shape on the surface of the sea:

a shoal of whales,   a flock of shearwaters,

a confluence of conflicting currents.

. . .

By then certain words had fallen out of service—

escalator, bus-strap, payslip.

By then Bell and Sigh had come to know the surface of the facing field as well as they knew the surfaces of the house: the cooker top that went from breakfast's coffee-pot to dinner's oil-slicked pans; the draining board that went from teaspoons and upturned cups to spatulas and full-moon plates.

The surface of the facing field, in summer, went from empty and lush to tousled and trampled, to chawed and sawed. The farmer came towing the fertiliser-spreading contraption. It pelted white pellets that the ground subsumed and after a couple of weeks the grass surged back.

By then Bell and Sigh were able to recognise a pasture anywhere, and know at once its past,   and tell its future.

There were ghost flies dithering in the dark

on the opposite side of the bathroom window as Bell and Sigh, elbow to elbow, brushed their teeth at night. And in the bedroom, a bockety square of light thrown onto the stained ceiling by the bedside lamp. And in the morning, shadows ebbing across the weathered floorboards as the sun met the scarves draped across the curtain rail that had remained undisturbed since the cooler days of earliest summer.

And in the bathroom, the soft-focused shapes of the yard through the lower, larger, frosted windowpane was a scene that had become as familiar to them as their own reflections in the double-sided, extendable shaving mirror. It was their sample of each day to come—the oblong of the van, the rectangle of the timber shed, the rock bank capped with a stripe of hedge and each shape's changing shade, depending upon the changing brightness—metallic red, tawny brown, grey and rich green.

Through the top window's unfrosted pane, the field hedge crested
into clarity, a crescendo of fuchsia, hawthorn, wild roses and flowering
briars, and the birds that tinkered in the crescendo—tits of three types,
a pair of chaffinches, the cantankerous robin.

The light,   in June,   like a rip current,
    sloshing across everything, sluicing out every crevice—
    the woodlice from beneath the skirting boards, the moths from
their wool folds, the ants from their hill.

At the far end of the concrete garden path, between gateposts,
there was a shallow saucepan filled with water—handleless, dinted—a
drinking-dish for Pip and Voss.

At clear noons, it caught the sun like a magnifying glass. It looked,
from the front-facing upstairs windows of the house, unlike a saucepan;
unlike a pool of water; unlike a refraction of the sun,
    but like a circular void, a hole drilled in the concrete with a fluid,
pearly substance fitfully spouting through;
                            like an opened eye,
    in which dazzled flies drowned.

Chapter Four

The mountain remained, unclimbed,
for the first four years that they lived there.

Unclimbed, as the soft leaves of the sycamore aged and toughened.

Unclimbed, as the thin rope of the washing-line frayed away and was replaced by one of steel wire with a coating of blue rubber,

                        like a slice cut through the sky.

Unclimbed, as the length of garden fence Bell and Sigh used as an overflow washing-line started to buckle beneath its inconstant burden of wet socks, to sag and sever into spikes.

Unclimbed, as a Lucozade bottle in the ditch at the mouth of the driveway endured, undamaged, for another full year—its garish label yellowing, its plastic hide puckering.

Unclimbed, as the surface of the double-sided, extendable shaving mirror above the bathroom sink filled up with four years of haphazardly flicked spit; as the magnifying side exaggerated every splatter and Bell's and Sigh's faces became swollen chimeras

        looming through

                a toothpaste snowstorm.

. . .

By their fifth July, all the windows of the house, inside and out, remained as unwashed as the mountain remained unclimbed.

On the out-facing glass—dry slime, grit and salt crystals.

On the in-facing glass—dust, webs, fingerprints, and at the precise
level of the small dog's head—a stippling of blobs painted by the tip of
his wet nose lightly,   earnestly   pressed.

A sideswipe here,   a smear,

the coda of his daily watching.

A new biscuit tin had been fitted into the groove flattened by its pre-
decessor. The faded sign had come unstuck; their old, full names lost.
The lid had rusted beyond use, until one night the wind carried it off.
The old tin had been Afternoon Tea. The new one was Elite Chocolate
Kimberly. And they never found the orphaned lid, though sometimes
they imagined they had seen it—sailing in a field puddle, glinting in the
post-storm sun; swinging from the neck of a spindly spruce like an aluminium medallion.

During the brightest months, woodlice, earwigs, centipedes and
beetles rushed to inhabit the dark box at the mouth of the driveway, the
cave-like cracks in the base of its rock.

Every time they checked for letters and found none, Bell or Sigh
made the same joke.

Look, they said. Somebody posted us bugs.

There had been just a few formal letters, in four years, and not a single
greeting card. The people who had once asked for their new address
had long since stopped asking. By then Bell and Sigh had successfully

completely lost touch with their large families, as discreetly as possible, dropping the odd call, and then all the calls. They had avoided confrontation at all costs; they had made as many hollow promises as they had to.

Outdoors, it was Sigh who took charge of the downward drag. He reattached the washing-line and reinforced the chicken wire. He glued the drooping seal of the front-facing door back into place. But Bell always helped when the recycling bin was blown over in the night; when they woke to the sound of toilet rolls reeling down the driveway, and to yoghurt pots capping the stems of the nettles like ludicrous puppets, and to sardine cans   sparring,

                                receipts limp with dew.

The oil man came at the start of every year with a fresh calendar. As each year progressed, the wisdoms it offered became increasingly strange and apathetic,   increasingly unwise.
    An open mouth catches no feet.
    Trying to define yourself is like trying to bite your own teeth.
    If you come to a fork in the road,   *take it.*

They stopped lighting the stove once all the leaves were out on the sycamore in June; this was their cue.
    Then the nightly ceremony of stove-lighting was replaced by a dusk douse in the icy sea. Each evening in the fading light, they waded out over the pebbles and sea peat, upsetting the beer-mat-sized flatfish with the soles of their feet.
    They dipped down and pushed off into the colder, calmer, bluer

stretches, swimming out for several backward strokes at most, several languid kicks, before returning again, to shore.

Weeds fondled their necks. Trout jumped to avoid them. Harmless jellyfish bumped against their bumps. They did it as a means of remembering their bodies; of being reminded that they were each made out of bodies—

skin rumpled, furrowed, knitted with hairs; nerves ending, cells circulating, chemicals responding.

They did it as a means of momentarily imperilling their habitually passive hides; of shocking away the sediment of unwarranted weariness that gathered inside their flaps and folds during the hours of stillness.

They did it as a means of remembering their surroundings; of being reminded that they were each made out of surroundings.

They swam clumsily; swam poorly; swam only on the brink of dark in entirely deserted places.

Everything about Sigh was ungainly and so were his strokes, but he covered ground, whereas Bell was ponderous and splashy. She swam as if skirmishing against the current. She boxed the waves she met head-on and booted the ones that snuck up behind. She made progress by ruining the placid surface.

For the purpose of swimming, they had fashioned suits, from a tank top, a T-shirt, a pair of footless tights, a pair of jeans with the legs lobbed off, and out of the centre of their largest bath towel, Bell had chopped a head-sized hole. She draped it over her shoulders, cape-like, as she dressed.

In the crannies of their toes, they carried crumbs of the beach home with them. Finely distributed between the carpet and the rugs, there was a dusting of sand, shale,

filaments of weed,
the carapaces of deceased sand-hoppers.

The farmer allowed the grass of the facing field to grow so long the blades swooned and keeled, leaning drunkenly into one another. Then he came in his tractor towing the hay-mower. He cut and left the grass laid out in stripes across the stubble for no more than two dry days. Then he turned and baled the sliced blades. Finally, the cows were allowed back to pick over the remnants, their tails listlessly swishing, as if disconnected from their bodies; as if being controlled by a single significant muscle positioned at the butt of the spine. Each time the muscles twitched, the rest of the tails followed suit. The switches swung involuntarily. They blew in the wind against each cow's will.

The pair of double duvets the dogs slept on had, by their fifth summer, begun to stink—of meat, feet, undergrowth—and so Bell and Sigh discussed the possibility of jamming them, one at a time, into the washing machine.

Sigh, on the side of washing them; Bell, against.

It will be like the runners, she said, it will only get worse.

July was the calmest month.

In their fifth year, there was a hooded crow who sat up on the unlidded chimney above the unlighted fire and dropped short twigs down the sooty shaft. Bell and Sigh heard the odd indignant caw, the ricocheting sticks and rattle of charcoal. They smelled the disturbed ash. They watched it flickering in the air of the sunlit living room.

Then a choir of flies piped up. A capricious zizzing that fazed the flickering dust of their warm, calm rooms.

After four summers, they were able to identify each species solely by the tenor of its buzz. There was the bass of a bloated bluebottle, the fizzle of a soprano mosquito, an ensemble of contralto houseflies. Though they hatched mainly downslope in the slurry of the farmer's slatted sheds, Bell and Sigh did not worry. They owned no swatter, dangled no sticky twists of paper. They released no insect-choking sprays.

The slurry-flies will strengthen our immune systems, Bell said, as did the kitchen tea-towel with its tremendous range of applications; as did the grimy dog bowls with their coating of russet-coloured mucus; as did the stinking duvets. And if ever either of them was fast enough to retrieve a morsel of dropped food before Voss had claimed it,

they ate it anyway,

and the hairs that were stuck to it,   the spores.

By then Bell and Sigh rarely came into contact with other humans and the ethereal repositories of airborne, touch-borne sicknesses they contained. In four years neither of them had suffered a single cough or cold or flu, a single stomach bug. The medications inside the bathroom cabinet—decongestants and anti-inflammatories, killers, quenchers and easers of assorted pain—had one by one reached and passed their expiration dates.

Blister packs had become separated from their boxes. Pills had become separated from their blister packs.

Instruction leaflets had been lost,

active ingredients deactivated.

. . .

One summer night they ventured out to test their immune systems, switching on the outside light above the kitchen door, casting new shadows across the boards of the bedroom where Pip and Voss had been left behind to wait. They descended the low hill, going in the lesser-travelled direction, toward the town. On foot it was twenty-five minutes to the closest pub. In the closest pub they sat in the corner furthest from the bar, which was encircled by small gatherings of local people, holiday-homers and caravaners, cautiously mingling, passing glasses, glances.

Bell and Sigh sat together, alone, and drank for as long as they could bear. In the open again, they inhaled deep draughts of mountain air, expelling the pestilence of strangers from their lungs,

exaggerating the gesture, becoming theatrical.

It was dark then, and they were lighter of step, skipping over the potholes, using as a guide the weak ray of the distant lamp above their kitchen door.

Only the white flowers were visible. Their pale faces breached the dark as if sliced from their stems, hovering like dim sparks.

Because the house was set back some hundred metres from the road, as soon as its lights had been switched off, it disintegrated into the field and sky, and if a person were to pass at night for the first time, they could not possibly know that   there   was

a house   there.

Back inside the disintegrated house,
they made attempts to touch the kitchen ceiling with the toes of their shoes. And out in the murky garden, they tried to balance on the pointed cusp of the concrete wall. They squatted down on the clammy

lawn and danced in what they believed to be the style of a Cossack: kicking up their heels at moths, tumbling back to jolt their tail-bones.

They teased the dogs, theatrically.

They swung, theatrically, in the tyre.

They never considered the possibility that one of them alone might catch a sickness and pass it on. All of their air was shared; all of their touches.

You get it I get it, they said. I get it you get it.

In the dark hall, the draught beneath the bedroom door created by the left-open window stirred Pip and Voss from sleep. It contained the stifled sounds and wispy scents of small beasts prowling, hunting, staking territory. Pip pressed her nose to the threshold. She sniffled and puffed. Voss raised his head and monitored the situation, softly growling.

In their fifth July, Bell resurrected the denim leg left over from the pair of jeans Sigh wore as swimming trunks. It had been put away inside a drawer of dislocated sleeves, hems and shirt collars. She sewed the hip up and he wadded it full of the other rags, and some kitchen-roll, the polyester floss of an ancient cushion. Then she sewed the foot up and laid it down to plug the crack.

But the draught-leg refused to slump; to form a dead weight between the floor and door. It should have been stuffed with sand or beans. Instead it was too light,   too pert.

The night,

its whispers and spice,

continued to leak past.

. . .

In the dark bedroom, after the cistern had finished replenishing, after the dogs had settled, after the night farming had finished, the sound of buzzing imposed itself upon the quietness.

Bell and Sigh played a guessing game with the choir of flies.

It was usually a daddy-long-legs—the scuffle of its cumbersome limbs caressing the plaster, sleazily. The amber, hirstute horsefly had a higher, nastier pitch, a blood-mustering bite. As soon as they heard it, Sigh climbed out of bed, blasted on the main light and reached for the slipper.

He clapped the walls. He shouted:

DO YOU SEE ANY FUCKING HORSES?

For the flies, time moved differently. Nights lasted weeks.

The sole of a raised slipper   took several hours
                                        to land.

Summer gales forced the swallows' second brood to fledge all together and too soon. Bell and Sigh woke to blunderous juveniles surfing the gusts,

          to a pair of looping choughs,

    to the farmer's dog barking far off, and close by, out in the hallway, their own dogs barking back, fidgeting and nibbling, combing the short fur of their paws with the sharp ends of their front teeth, waiting,

          always waiting,

                              for Bell and for Sigh.

Neither of them could remember, then, which dog had belonged to whom first.

Nor who had once been responsible for the carton of semi-skimmed milk at the very back of the freezer, the unopened jar of rhu-

barb jam in the cupboard of dog food; nor who had misplaced the
plastic cap of the gear stick, the SCART lead for the DVD player, the
egg-whisk; nor who had first made a feature of lining the windowsills
with second-hand books, of keeping the toilet rolls in a pyramid on the
top of the cistern, of stacking the multicoloured bowls in four shallow
piles on the kitchen shelf.

The time for rearranging crockery had passed.

It was   by then   inconceivable
that a plate or mug or bowl might appear somewhere other than in
its place.

It was   by then   inconceivable
that there would not be a bar of green soap in the left-side soap-
nook of the bathroom sink, wearing slowly away, losing its perfect oval
shape, becoming enmeshed with hairs and sand,

              paling and subsiding into sludge.

They saw that one of the fledgling swallows was a ghost. The feathers
across the back of its open wings had failed to develop into the charcoal
blue of its siblings. Instead its body was patchy white, and its face was
tawny, like a sepia photograph.

Their fifth summer brought a spell of rainless heat that lasted so long
the intimately known ditches became

                          unrecognisable—
parched beyond recognition—the fronds singed, the green leaves
scorched orange. The dogs' piss rolled the dust and evaporated. Above
the unfamiliar ditches, clutches of cinnabar moths levitated.

At night Bell and Sigh could only muster sleep with their arms and

legs stuck out from beneath the thinnest blanket. They lay so carefully.
They lay without touching each other and without allowing any part of
their skin to rest against a different, adjacent part. Throughout the heat
wave, they woke intermittently to flip the pillows, to grope with their
feet for cooler pockets of sheet. They got up and stood on the bath-mat
in front of the sink splashing their sweaty limbs with water.

Afraid of not being able to sleep at all,

    they swam for longer. They swallowed a magnitude of sea air. They
existed as intensely as possible in order to exhaust themselves.

They lit a fire in a bucket and stayed up late. On the barest ground of
the most sheltered side of the house, they rolled out the dog duvets and
wrapped up fillets of fish in tinfoil, corn on the cobs and baked potatoes, and blackened and smoked them between the coals.

    They lay down and studied the heavens for passing bats,

satellites,

meteor showers.

Too hot   to walk the dogs by day, due to the heavy wool coats
they could never take off. Walks became sluggish pilgrimages to and
from the emerald stream late in the evening. Voss stepped in first,
dipping the bulge of his chest, his monstrous tongue lapping. Pip followed, submerging as much of her wool as possible. She spread herself
across the slippery bed, groaning, stemming the current. She shattered
the protective cases of the caddisfly larvae. She soaked the water beetles up.

. . .

Too hot   for them to leave the dogs in the van while they were in
the supermarket, and so they shut them in the bedroom;
                    this was the room they chose,
    for its changeable view of the field. They left the window open wide
enough to provide a trickle of sensorial stimulants, but not so wide that
Voss might be inspired to wriggle and fall his way free. In the supermarket,   they rushed,
    neglecting to consult their list, forgetting essential items, select-
ing needless replacements. They arrived home with a tin of spiced kip-
pers when what they had needed was plain salmon; with a tub of comb
honey when what they had needed was squeezy; with a bottle of personalised Coke,   an artichoke.
    You know they dress up in our clothes when we're not there, Sigh
said. And do our voices.

The mountain knew   that Pip and Voss
    only waited   for Bell and for Sigh   to come back.
    Sometimes Voss worked on the incremental destruction of his
chicken-flavour-infused Nylabone. Sometimes Pip plucked out the
wings of the window-trapped flies with her tiny incisors.

Too hot   for the flowering grasses to moulder and wilt. Instead
they desiccated, turning to straw. Bell picked them from the banks of
the driveway and bound them into bouquets with elastic bands. She
poked their pointed stalks into the compost of the potted plants, sow-
ing their rooms with frozen flames.

. . .

By the third and final week of drought, the elastic bands had started to pop. The stream had almost come to a stop.

Its bed was clogged by thirsty weeds: water mint, brooklime, angelica.

They drove to the peninsula to spare the dogs a hot slog and carried a bottle of water and a tin dish along the cliff path, inside a cloth bag with a long strap that clanked like a cowbell with every step. Or they forgot the bag, and Sigh wore the dish like a helmet.

Red soldiers crowded on to the flowering hogweed.

The dogs kept a slack pace, panting, and what remained of the stream ran copper-coloured, drawing iron ore up from the sedimentary rocks. The cleft it had sawed became a bright slash bleeding out, brilliantly, into the sea.

At last, it rained again.

The greenery gradually reconstituted.

Julys faded their caps and canvas runners
    to the colours of whatever happened to be closest—
            to lawn green, sand yellow, cloud grey.

Julys tanned the backs of their hands and wrists, bringing up new freckles. They held them out and reached down and compared them to the paleness of their feet.

They saved up the final plant of their sacrosanct potato crop, in the same way they left the best fruit in the bowl to rot.

The final potatoes became engulfed by warts, by rust. Beneath the mud-lid, they macerated and mutated.

Bell and Sigh argued—in their fifth year as they had in their first—over the season in which August fell.

Sigh, on the side of summer; Bell, on the side of autumn.

Young dunnocks frisked the bracken, diving beneath its mesh but continuing to call.

Along their road there was a hump of rock that resembled, on approach, a white cat crouching. On a pale slab in a low wall, there was a dark stain that formed the silhouette of a rabbit poised on its hind legs. There was a gorse branch where a blackbird perched—

a blackbird sculpted out of wood by the angle of the sun.

There was the trawler-box trough, the picnic bench, the clump of creeping ivy, the gap and the smudge, the hole in the island of rock. There was the corpse of the ornamental cabbage, wrinkled to death by drought. There was an extravagance of meadowsweet.

Bell and Sigh pointed them out to each other:

the familiar things, again; the unfamiliar, anew.

They plucked the hirsute buds off the knapweed they passed and rolled them between their fingers.

If they had stopped and calculated how far they walked each evening and all the evenings they had walked, they would have found that

by then

they'd be in Ottawa,   Ankara,

if only they had kept going west, east

instead of repeatedly

turning   back.

Swallows dive-bombed the clustered bullocks, pitching off the power lines, plunging for flies.

The ghost had been butchered by a buzzard on its third day of flight.

A dead cow jounced past in the bucket of the farmer's digger. Legs rigid in the air, hoofs spilling, udders ablaze.

The means by which the cows came to be lying down was incomprehensibly awkward. It involved a calculated collapsing of limbs, a sink, a plonk. The skimpiness of their legs seemed, to Bell and to Sigh, like a mistake; for just four short, knobbled, tapering limbs to be responsible for the support of a ton of ambling beast. Their scuffed hip bones jutted out even though they were fat—pinning up their hides like tent poles, leaving their overloaded guts to sag,   to swing.

The cows were vastly mysterious.

The farmer was vastly mysterious.

To him each cow was intimately known, entirely pedestrian. His face was red in summer and purple in winter. He hung no net curtains; arranged no figurines upon the road-facing sills of his farmhouse, no flower vases, no books,

no candlesticks,   no model sailing ships.

He wore a white linen shirt as he drove the tractor. He wore it as he herded and milked and calved. All year round his shirts remained miraculously unsullied and perpetually untucked, tails tossing loose in the breeze. He braked every time he met Bell and Sigh on the road. He wound down the driver's window and talked about what the weather was and had been and would be. He told them who had died or might soon. He commented on the fluctuating phone reception.

They had heard that the farmer kept a father in the house with him, ancient and shuffling and bent, who bought the newspaper every morning, but read only the obituaries.

They had heard that the farmer didn't eat or sleep or shave or use

the toilet; that he had no cause for any of the routine expurgations or
ablutions of an ordinary, weak human body.

They had heard that the farmer was descended from pirates.

He offered to help Bell and Sigh with anything,
with everything.

In the garden Voss barked at a suspicion.

The bark bounced off a rock peak and echoed, and he barked back
at his echo and so on, reminding Bell and Sigh of how they still had not,
in four years and seven months,
climbed.

How they might have been in southern Ontario, in Central Anatolia,
by then, if things had been different. Instead they had not even
climbed.

A fetid puddle surrounded the drain outside the kitchen door—an oily
soup of the traces of once-eaten substances. It trickled a miniature
curdled river down the driveway, meandering around the lady's bed-
straw and lesser hawkbit, drowning the shamrock. The sun could not
seem to vaporise it, and there had been no rain strong enough to sluice
it away.

The landlord was called to unblock the drain. He came armed with
rods and rubber gloves. As he crouched on the gravel to rummage and
bail, Sigh finally remembered to ask him about the mountain—whether
or not it was commonage, and if there was a path all the way to the top.
Yes and yes, he told them, though it was probably overgrown because
nobody went up there. The mouth of the path was through the farmer's

yard behind the milking parlour and he himself had never climbed it, though for a long time he had been meaning to.

They say there is a wild goat who lives up there, the landlord said, the last surviving member of an indigenous flock.

They say that from the top, the landlord said, you can see seven standing stones, seven schools,
and seven steeples.

Pip chased the white cat.
Pip chased the black cat.

The cats changed colour as they ran—their patterns blurred and re-configured, unknitted and reknitted, transformed—

becoming brown-striped as they streaked through brambles, flickering into green as brambles met bracken. Sometimes the cats happened upon small hawthorns, elders, willows and clawed their way up to the highest, thickest branches, and Pip halted at the bottom and pawed the earth. She whined and jumped. She glowered into the canopy until hours had passed; until night was starting; until she had forgotten what she was doing there beneath the hawthorn or elder or willow in the half-dark. Eventually she went home, lapped up a dish of tinned fish, boiled potato skins and wet bread. Eventually she prostrated herself, dog-weary, across the hearthrug. And Bell and Sigh knelt in front of the unlighted fire to pinch the thorns from her scooping chest, to comb for ticks.

Blood on Pip's soft ears and in the corners of her black-rimmed eyes, her arteries hammering.

. . .

She had come to know that gardens were where they lived:

                                                                        the cats.

She hesitated at every gate, squinting through its bars. She scanned the
yard and lawn, the decking and the flower-beds, the windowsills and
shrubbery, the fiberstone Buddhas and robotic lawn-mowers.

Sometimes she killed a cat, grudgingly—disappointed that it had
spoiled their game of chase

                                              by getting caught.

The tick tower on top of the kitchen fridge continued to rise.

Some summers the ticks were prolific; others, they were scarce.

Some summer nights Bell or Sigh sat on the lowered lid of the toilet as the other failed to fully tweezer an embedded tick free from the
tensed flesh of an ankle or belly or thigh. Then they lay awake clenching their eyelids, picturing a house plagued by ticks—ticks pinging
out of curtain folds and cushion covers, ticks scampering up from the
cracks between boards, ticks spattering down from faucets. They pic-
tured themselves trying to herd the whole plague back into a single,
small container that they then repeatedly knocked to the floor

and watched   helplessly   as it poured.

In August they would return to the same spot every couple of days for
mackerel, to a recess in the limestone cliff face at the low end of the
peninsula. It was wide as a porch with sides high enough to enclose the
dogs. Strands of old rope and kelp stalks snagged and crisped across
the scabrous rocks. Auks paddled past. Herring gulls wise to Bell and

Sigh's routine kept watch for the littering of guts and off-cuts. They lunged.

And a bull seal waited beneath the surface until several fish were hooked at once. Then he scooted from the shadows, intercepting the line, stealing as many shimmering bodies as he could in the space of seconds with only his teeth.

Bell and Sigh murdered the fish by thwacking their heads against the rocks. A single hard crack and the life shuddered out in aftershocks.

When they were just a few hours dead, the halved mackerels spasmed in the hot frying pan. They curled,
    recoiling against the scorching oil   as if half-alive.

Bell and Sigh wore sunglasses, not just in the town but in the kitchen, in the evenings, hunched over the frying pan as the fresh fish spat tiny, scalding bullets of oil.

The holiday homes had come alive by then—with the beating out of the holiday rugs and holiday curtains; with the buffing of dust from the holiday trinkets. Late in the mornings, the coastline sang with the sound of coffee machines breaking back into churring, pittering life, and in the afternoons Bell and Sigh met the holiday men incompetently fishing.

They knew him by his polypropelene folding stool, and his spangling set of virgin tackle: a reel of gleaming monofilament, the iridescent feathers of peahens, kingfishers, hummingbirds. He cast out with a catastrophic lack of technique into a reef, a morass of weed, the bull seal.

How Bell and Sigh—in their cliff-gashed raincoats, with the sides of their canvas runners rending loose from the soles and the sleeves

of their sweaters smeared with mackerel blood, and their salt-matted mongrels—hated the man with two homes, who owned a hundred
things he did not use; who had a duplicate holiday set of his hundred
unused things.

Four years and seven months passed without a single visitor.

There had been a couple of casual enquiries that they received with
dread, with grim seriousness, and after intricate discussion, agreed to
ignore.

By then   Bell and Sigh were no longer able to bear the prob-
ability that their most precious assemblages—the Elrond shrine, the
spectacle of succulents, the hoard of bald tennis balls—might appear to
an old friend as clutter at best and chaos at worse; that they might lay
bare the most splendid aspects of their splendid universe—the sycamore in maximum leaf, the thistles in superlative flower, the everlasting
potato, the unclouded panorama—to find that the old friend perceived
all of these things—any one of these things—to be completely unre-
markable.

By then   they struggled to remember whether old friends
might be perturbed by a tea-stained mug, or several layers of oil burned
into the base of a baking tin and bits of the blackened tin flaking into
the food as it baked, or the head of a large, salt-matted mongrel lying in
their lap as they ate, a small, salt-matted mongrel staring at them, drib-
bling on the toes of their shoes.

By then   they could not bear the idea of having to throw away
the debris of a meticulously prepared meal. Old friends, as far as they
could remember, tended to leave a couple of mouthfuls of food behind on the surface of their plate—sometimes spread lightly, sometimes
heaped up at a single point—whereas Bell and Sigh always finished

every morsel and scraped the china with the tines of their forks and placed their plates down on the rug for the dogs to glaze with drool.

In their fifth August, they solved the problem of their old friends by each buying a new SIM card.

In Bell's new contacts list, she saved Sigh's number.

In Sigh's new contacts list, he saved Bell's number.

The driveway was so overgrown by the end of Augusts that they would duck to avoid the thwacking greenery even when they were encapsulated by the van. As the wrists and tips of the hedge smacked the backs of the wing mirrors and twanged the aerial,

they ducked.

The van's left side, as they drove, became drily buttered with dust and viciously scribbled by the passing ditches. Left behind on the red steel, every journey they'd made since the last spell of heavy showers had left its unintelligible signature.

Red-hot pokers which they had not planted appeared in a clump at the end of the driveway—nine fireworks mounted atop the green trail of their ascent, nodding an ominous welcome.

The lilies, which they hadn't planted either, bowed their discoloured bonnets and stuck out their bloated, orange tongues as a beacon to the hover-flies that crawled inside and supped the last of the lily juice. The cones had fantastic acoustics. A gentle, guzzling buzz became the chatter of a cassette player on fast-forward.

There was a sense of hysteria amongst the insects.

In the evening, in the garden, Bell and Sigh watched a red-tailed bee build a nest inside the concrete wall. It was a new queen. First she nibbled a cloth of leaf from the wild rose bush. Then she flew it back to her chosen hollow, cradled beneath her abdomen as if riding a magic carpet. Then she folded it, daintily, through the narrow entrance. Each time there was a pause while out of sight the new queen trimmed, pleated and upholstered. Finally she re-emerged and returned to the wild bush of roses, to nibble a new cloth.

The concrete wall, they realised, was a warren of hollows,

> a man-made hive,

>> an insect skyscraper.

Not alone the bee, but woodlice, ants, earwigs and spiders made their homes in different grey apartments on different crumbling storeys of the garden high-rise.

The last task every night was to let the dogs out into the garden so that Voss could empty his bladder and Pip—about whom everything was elongated, lagging, tempered, even the filtration of water through her organs and its transformation into piss—could stand obstructing the doorway, sniffing the propitious dark.

In the propitious dark, the insects were even more hysterical.

As soon as the field-facing door of the house opened, moths hurled themselves into the rectangle of brightness and branched out between rooms, hurrying, in search of glowing bulbs.

When the moths found the bulbs, they never seemed sure what to do. They tried to get as close as possible. They fondled the wafer-thin glass with their friable antennae, awestruck. They basked on the ceiling inside the realm of its warmth.

Across the insect skyscraper, across the driveway,

across the fields, the cattle road, the gorse,
every night,
the mountain saw the door of the house rupture into a sultry portal.
Through the black quagmire of moths, it saw
an opening,   eye-like.

Chapter Five

The mountain remained, unclimbed,
for the first five years that they lived there.

Downslope, things continued to build up.

The words they had spoken to each other built up, and the millions
of sentences that contained them, stretching back through their years,
uncounted, as did the countless steps they'd taken, the miles they'd
driven, the gallons of water they'd flushed through their cistern and
poured down their plug holes,   their throats.

The compost in their bin built up. The magnets on their fridge
blocked out the white. Their charity-shop clothes—old even before Bell
and Sigh had bought them—built up, until one day they filled a sack for
the recycling centre. They threw every jumper, skirt and shirt out onto
the bed-cover. They re-evaluated every pattern; questioning whether
certain colour combinations had since become garish, or certain shapes
unflattering, or certain styles unsuited to the slightly different selves
they had since become.

The smells built up—the dog duvets, the damp and soot, the oils ex-
creted by the frying of oily fish, the smoulder of sandalwood, cedarwood

and eucalyptus-scented joss-sticks—all together stewing into a perfume
of their own:

the smell of the house;

the smell of their days.

The rash of mildew on the bathroom wall had, by their sixth August,
been painted over three times. The washing machine filter had been
changed twice; the bag for the swing bin two hundred. But the battery
for the smoke alarm had never been renewed and neither Bell nor Sigh
could remember precisely when it had stopped chirping.

A snarl of hay and fur had four times been swept out of the bathroom extractor fan and still the starlings came back every spring to
nest, as the mildew came back every winter, looming through the new
white,   intensifying into sight.

All the scissors were blunted then, as was the lonely kitchen knife.
Sigh bought a fine-grained whetstone and enthusiastically sharpened
every blade-like thing he found in the cutlery drawer, the tackle box.

He sharpened three of the longest dog sticks into spears.

He sharpened even the chicken-flavour-infused Nylabone.

Their teeth were blunted too, by then, broached by pinprick holes,
sketched by hairline cracks. All day they licked out their respective cavities, unconsciously. By the force of their insistent tongues and the cor-
roding acids and sugars they ate, the cavities deepened, widened—from
pinprick to pinhead to the size of a particle.

Newer, bigger pieces of food became lodged with greater frequency.

. . .

In the shorn, tight, teal pile of the carpet on the stairs, other kinds of particles had become lodged.

The carpet on the stairs was the sole fixed-down surface. It could never be uprooted, flung across the garden wall and flagellated. In their sixth year, they bought a second-hand hoover. It had lost a wheel and most of its nozzles. It was cheap but weak—too weak to conquer five full years' worth of the eclectic grit that had collected in the carpet on the stairs—the microscopic fibres of pine needles and pollen, sand and shale, splinters and mud. The carpet on the stairs contained the beach and wood and field and mountain. It clutched the smallest particles of their years. Though Bell would occasionally, on bended knee, assault it with the crevice-shaped nozzle—prodding and scraping—the teal pile only ever ceded its top layer.

By early autumn the house teemed with insects.

There were the moths that entered last thing at night and tucked themselves into the pockets of cardigans. There was an earwig Sigh carried around in his shoe for an entire day, unharmed, and a mosquito that ravaged Bell in her sleep, a dozen bites from scalp to crotch. There was a posse of fruit-flies suspended above the compost bucket like fat dots of floating, vibrating dust. There was a black slug the size of a mouse that criss-crossed the kitchen rug at night, the streak of its slime tracing the outlines of the imitation oriental symbols: a star, a peony, the tree of life.

What we need, Sigh said, is a kitchen hedgehog.

By early autumn the population of bedroom flies would reach crisis point. All night they circuited the ceiling in a throng;

one by one dizzying,   tiring,   straggling away,

only to become ensnared

by the morass of cobwebs in the wall-crevasse directly above Bell and Sigh's pillows.

Directly above the place where they laid their heads to sleep at night, queen spiders feasted. Discarded wings fluttered down to settle on their eyelashes, or became lost between the strands of their outspread hair, or inhaled, ingested. Moths climbed into the downy nooks of their ears, guided by the motes of light from their brains.

They woke to the deafening scuffle of wings, or to a chorus of distressed buzzing—the death throes of the night flies,

silk-strangled,   partially engorged.

They disputed which species of house pest they'd prefer to feel running across their face at night.

Sigh, on the side of spiders; Bell, on the side of mice.

A shield bug drowned at dawn in the bedside water glass they shared. Hours later Bell drank the green-tinged water from around it. She took three sips before her dream-addled mind registered a strange taste, the faintly astringent flavour of fear pheromones.

Maybe you will have superpowers now, Sigh said.

The power to remain asleep all winter, unfed.

The power to draw the sap of a leaf without causing any damage to the plant.

The power to fall from a height ten times the length of your body and remain completely unharmed.

. . .

They watched a music festival on the deteriorating TV set, late at night. Across the rag-rug and the hearthrug, across the huddle of mantelpiece-facing figurines assembled on the TV sideboard, across an enormous, rain-soaked human crowd twinkling with cigarette lighters and the up-raised illuminated screens of six-and-a-half-thousand mobile phones,

    there was a floodlit stage, a tiny woman singing about infatuation,
                             avarice,   and loss.
They watched greyhound racing, after the music festival had ended. They sat, hypnotised by the throttling dogs. Each one kept inside their given track, oblivious to the others, to the loudspeakers and the human crowds. Only the mechanical lure existed for them—a soft toy between a rail and a wire rope, two seconds faster than the fastest dog.

In their sixth August, at varied stages of the evening, they watched the Olympics. They debated the different bodies and how each had been chiselled into its distinctive shape by a set of rules and repeated tricks: the thick-shouldered rowers, the flipper-footed swimmers, the needle-legged long-distance runners. They considered the sportsper-son's brains—singularly devoted to the execution of a vault or flip or hurdle, to the fastest straight line swam, the steadiest wide circle ran, to the most exquisite splash—

    to the ability to fall from a height ten times the length of a body and remain completely unharmed.

The TV reception had suffered, over the years, at the hands of the sec-ond most prevalent wind. Easterlies toyed with the aerial,
    tweaking it,   prising it
        gently,   spitefully,
further and further out of its original position until the pictures splin-tered   and tripped   and stuttered.

The screen was already frosted with dust.

Through the lint and smuts and static, they were still able to decipher enough movement and sound to construct a narrative. They spoke over everything they watched, guessing at storylines, recounting new versions, piecing back together the meteorologist's map, the vacillating credits, the jumping parts of a half-remembered face.

The blue chiffon moon of early autumn
belonged to them, the last of the sycamore leaves, the meadowsweet,
the bees,   all theirs.

The foliage of the fuchsia fell from the bush before the flowers. The flowers held on like tiny armless men in purple tutus, half a dozen skinny legs each. The last of the bees worked urgently, rummaging amongst the legs. The music they made in unison was a luscious, industrious vibrato.

Bell picked the last of the bees, along with the fuchsia, and carried them inside. By then there were a great many empty glass bottles to choose from: green, blue, brown,
    rectangular, pot-bellied, tapering,
    apple cider, balsamic vinegar, elderflower cordial.

The gold spandex sun of early autumn
shot the sharpest of its evening rays into the magnifying side of the bathroom shaving mirror. They bounced back and hit the window, circulating the whiff of smoking vinyl, melting a mess of black pocks in the vinyl frame. Sigh suggested they paint the backside of the mirror black, or cover it with a circle of custom-cut card. But they didn't. Instead they draped the bathroom hand towel over the window-facing side of

the mirror every time they had to leave the house, and if they forgot, they would panic;

they would rush back.

It became another of the small domestic threats that haunted their abbreviated necessary absences. There was the threat of the immersion heater left switched on; the threat of a convector radiator covered with a damp towel; the threat of a disc-shaped hob glowing a burning orange through the abandoned kitchen,   as if it was

an early autumn sun.

They had planned, in the beginning, to furnish only provisionally. No additional shelving, they had agreed, no new appendages to the fabric of the house. Nothing painted, nothing installed, nothing screwed down—in order that they would never, at short notice, have to screw up, to de-install, to un-paint.

Instead   everything draped, propped, hung,
                                    heaped, dropped, slung.

In each of their respective pasts, circumstances had insisted upon falling apart when Bell and Sigh had least expected it, and it followed, they agreed, that life would surely hold together so long as they remained, constantly,   prepared.

Inside their rooms the draped, dropped, propped, hung, slung and heaped things they co-owned defied them. As the years passed, the individual objects collected swelled and embedded.

The scarves knotted their tassels around the curtain rail. The pictures sank through the white emulsion and into the plaster. The turquoise arabesques of their best throw blanket wove into the twisted script of the Latin sofa. The spindly roots of the plants clawed out through the perforated soles of their pots, pierced their allocated surfaces and burrowed, gathering strength, penetrating the timber-imitation lino, the wood boards, all the way down to the concrete foundations of the house.

They had imagined, in the beginning, that if everything they owned was old and shoddy, even ugly, certainly nearing the end of its useful life, then they would better be able to bear its loss.

Instead the past and passing years softened their pity into affection. They grew fond of their crappy, useless stuff. It became, to Bell and to Sigh,

> precious.

They lived in a kind of retirement.
They lived as if they were their own precious stuff—

> nearing the useful end of life.

They mentioned money only cursorily, as if it was a concern from some other, earlier era, irrelevant then; the concern of some community they were no longer a part of.

The right leg of Sigh's grey corduroy trousers finally ripped open, and so he bent over and drew a smiling face in blue biro, upside down, on the cap of his cold knee.

His safety boots were not in great shape either. The suspension was gone. The toes had caved in. They wafered, unsafely, at the seams.

They make me look like a man who has been ravaged by pit bulls, Sigh said. No. Worse. They make me look like the kind of man who stole them from a man who'd been ravaged by pit bulls—who was lying on the ground, shouting for help—but instead of helping him,

I stole his shoes
and ran away.

In one sense, they were ancient.
    In another sense, they were adolescent,
              or even   infantile.

It was not long before they raided the black sack of old clothes they
had put aside for recycling but never brought to the centre. They threw
everything out onto the bed-cover again. They picked back through to
decide which garish colours, unflattering shapes and unsuitable styles
were not so bad as they remembered.

Out on the peninsula, when it was calm, stone-washed butterflies
spewed from the heather, painted ladies that had flown all the way
from southern Europe to escape a drought. When it was wild, Voss's
wind-blown coat—his tattered, red-tinted black curls—was de-tattered
and uncurled by the volleys of wind.
    Voss ate the kindling, the clinkers, the rags moulted by the most-
worn rugs. In the bathroom, when no one was watching, he licked drop-
lets of piss from the tile-imitation lino. In the kitchen, even when they
were watching, he licked spatters of cooking oil from the oriental rug.
    He had become fastidious about vomiting. He understood that he
must aim for the naked patches of floor if he was to avoid being rep-
rimanded. First he hawked up the irritant fragment. Then he did his
best to reclaim any lost food—lapping the frothy broth of fishy bile and

soggy grass stalks, leaving behind a shard of stick or plastic toy, a peel of raw potato.

Both dogs needed new collars. The good leather of their original collars had gone bad, dull and stiff. Voss needed a new harness as well as a collar. His original harness had frayed around the links. Its rubber lining lifted away from the inside of the straps

in chips and scraps.

He was a hard-wearing dog and his accessories suffered, whereas Pip was gentle and faltering. Her shackles of all forms withstood her pace of life.

At her most majestic, out on the peninsula, Pip stood up straight and reared her head to deeply sniff; her ears pricked; her flesh stretched across her scooping ribcage, fluttering in time with the flaring of her nostrils. Inside the house, she was meek and unreadable again.

Bell and Sigh put a lot of effort into deducing Pip's emotional state. They reassured her as often as they could, and castigated Voss as often as they had to. When the dogs pursued a smell, they pursued the dogs. They rushed forward, together but out of time. They rocketed, stumbled, zig-zagged, through thickets, gullies, heath. They stopped shy of the cliff's edge as the trail petered out

into rubble,   then sea.

They went to the vet every autumn.

Every autumn, in the surgery, the vet revised what age the dogs might be. He checked the condition of their gums. He counted their grey and greying whiskers. He listened to the rhythmic squidging of their chests.

Most years Pip and Voss measurably declined, but there were also
years when they seemed to have stopped growing older or even to have
grown younger; their greyness receding, gums plumping, pulses surging
back. Then the vet crossed out the approximated dates of birth in their
vaccination booklets, and put down new numbers, guessing a new age,
replacing the old guess.

In September the nights finally cooled. Bell put away her swimming
cape and their salt-damaged suits. The stove was re-lit. The insects that
had become trapped inside the house in summer commenced to hiber-
nate   or to die.
    Woodlice littered the thresholds, rocking on their straked backs like
clinker-built rowboats. Dead moths adorned the lapels of Bell's and
Sigh's jumpers like crumbling brooches. The disarticulated parts of flies
dusted the windowsills, bluebottles still whole and twitching. A centi-
pede lay in the bottom of the log basket with every leg curled inward,
hugging itself exactly forty-four times.
    Only the queen spiders survived. They were huge and languid then,
fattened by the fly-bounty of summer, tame. Occasionally they left
the morass of cobwebs in Bell and Sigh's bedroom to pay a visit to the
ground level of the house. They trotted, brazenly, out into the centre of
the hearthrug. They fixed their gaze to the jumping static of the deteriorating TV, eight unblinking eyes each.

September dawns, a slew of light on the bedroom ceiling, moving like
the dregs of a translucent drink   swilled
                              around the bottom of a tumbler.
    In the distance there was the sound of an excavator: the wrangle of

hydraulics, the jangle of links and cylinders, the clatter of bucket and boom. It was scraping the topsoil from the fields, carrying it away and dumping it elsewhere. It was rearranging the scenery, such that the distance came slowly closer, approaching,

            such that new,   small mountains grew.

By afternoon the land left behind was a desert of boulders and wan mud.

            And gulls,

like paper aeroplanes,   like kites

dipping and revolving, tethered to the desert by translucent strings. The racket they made was the shrill, wailing siren for an air raid. It could be heard from every room of the house, dampening the hooded crow's grudging croaks. Every upstairs window seemed to sit at the same height as the gulls soared, and so their listless winging dabbed out the dirty blue plains of sky.

To the branches of the sycamore—from the vantage of the upstairs windows—yellow lichens gripped, and more green algae than green foliage.

The leaves had begun to brown,

            their tips nipped by the cooling nights.

The walls flanking their road would be rickety were it not for the flora that plugged each hollow—bindweed, pennywort, creeping ivy—and the moss and turf clasping each stone in place.

In spring and summer, briars and gorse engineered a scaffold. In autumn and winter, the walls were robbed of their reinforcements; the wind hissed through their holes again, toppling the odd stone.

Blackberries blotted the scaffolds. Ragwort speared up. In the night their tall stems appeared to uproot from the ditches surrounding the

cattle fields; to toss themselves across the road and lie there, trampled: petals limp, roots drooped.

Hubcaps appeared between the ferns and murdered ragwort—with
six thick, rigid plastic spokes, an archaic symbol embossed at the heart.
Bell and Sigh pointed the hubcaps out to each other, and all the familiar things, again;

and every unfamiliar thing,

anew.

In the beginning, they had argued in their completely unargumentative
way over the bad bits in the broccoli. Sigh believed that a single rot-
ten floret rendered the whole head ruined, whereas Bell spared as much
good broccoli as possible, eating traces of the black and yellow along
with the green.

She would ask him what he would like for dinner and he would
say he didn't mind, or he would ask her what she would like for dinner and she would say she didn't mind. And dinner was always the
same anyway, on a seven-day rotation, subject to incidental varia-
tion—the weather, the time they arrived home from the evening walk,
the fish that had been caught, or not, the surplus or dearth of certain vegetables. Seven dinners was all that they knew; all that they
shopped for. Sometimes a bargain pineapple, in the spirit of fru-
gality, or a celeriac, in the spirit of experiment, appeared in the
fridge,   later to be abandoned—
first to slacken, then to discolour, eventually to fester.

The kitchen cooker had responded to their rotation of dinners
in the order of how it fell apart. The knobs corresponding to their
most-used hobs were the first to drop off. Then the fan of the over-
used oven tired and slowed, taking two minutes, five minutes, ten

minutes more to roast the parboiled potatoes, to raise the beaten eggs.

The opposite sides of the house were two separate ecosystems.

Often it drizzled, or there was a rainbow, or an aeroplane passed on one side but not the other.

Because the two large windows of the living room were set directly opposite one another, it was possible to stand on the rock-facing side of the house and see straight through to the sea-facing side though the view was obscured by the unwashed panes, the trinkets, books and plants crowding the sills. As the sun slithered down behind the rock, its shadow slithered up the surface of the front-facing field: a rectangle topped by the slant of the pitched roof, a chimney either end like a pair of horns;

the bright blanks of the downstairs windows and the clouds that charted across the dirty glass.

The mountain could look straight through too, both ways,

from field to rock; from rock to field.

They parked the van on the rock-facing side. In bad weather they pulled up as tightly as possible to the kitchen door, hugging the un-painted plaster, flattening the dead herbs.

The van broke down, at different moments, in different ways. The engine sneezed and palpitated, struggling to climb hills. The battery suddenly shuddered and died. The wipers stopped and refused to start again, and then it rained for days.

Vantastic, they would say.

. . .

They had grown accustomed to disrepair.

They had come to believe that it was not possible for everything to work at once. As soon as one thing was fixed, something else would break. This was their cosmic balance.

Though they still had not reached an agreement on the designation of doors, they would always know what portal the other was referring to— and which dog or condiment or TV station; which piece of cutlery or clothing or fruit—without having to name it.

Theirs was a language of overtones and allusions,

of gentle shunts,

nods,   grunts.

By then they had compromised on the broccoli. Sigh silently placed the tainted head down; Bell dissected it.

A diamante of fish skin,

sprinkled in the curls of Voss's black back.

He stood too close to the sink as Sigh shaved each fillet in preparation for baking, and too close to the red-hot door of the stove in the evenings, and too close to the traffic that passed.

He wore the scales of the pollock and a minuscule spinach leaf everywhere he went for four days, glued to his hairy chin with spit.

Dew drops, aphids, larvae, grains of rice and coarse flour, flakes of garlic skin, tissue, bran. Voss, like the carpet on the stairs, held a microscopic material archive within his ragged coat.

. . .

Like Voss, like the carpet on the stairs, Bell and Sigh gathered fragments of their environment: a blob of toothpaste on a collar first thing in the morning, a drip of soup in the lap later on, a sediment of mud sucked up from the wet cliff path ringing each trouser cuff. They wore them like badges of the day so far, of yesterday and the day before.

They wore each other's hair inside their socks and up their sleeves: long, light, nuttish-brown lengths.

Their hair was the same colour then, and neither of them could re-member   whether or not   it had always been that way.

A pink buoy on a blue rope appeared on the beach at low tide. It was anchored to a lobster pot on the seabed. '

Voss noticed it at once.

At once he wanted to possess it; to add it to his compendium of balls. Every low tide he tried to drag it up. At first he couldn't force his jaws to fit around its pink girth, but after a spot of aggressive gnawing, the polyform plastic burst and he was able to collapse it between his teeth, to ram it right the way back to his molars.

Voss stood on the last stretch of uncovered sand, at the furthest ex-tension of his extendible leash, five full metres from the handle—teeth clamped, back paws half-sunk, front paws pushing, levering—he yanked the squashed plastic.

With every muscle of his whole small body, he yanked. As his hocks and tail and rump disappeared into the wet sand, he yanked. As the ris-ing tide eddied around his pigeon chest.

Voss knew he must drag the lobster buoy up from the sea, or the lobster buoy would drag Voss

into   the sea.

. . .

By-the-wind sailors bobbed past the moored, punctured buoy and set-tled on the sea peat and rough sand. A dozen venemous jellyfish came in on the same tide. Each was a sealed, frilled pocket of air, no big-ger than an inflated condom. Each trailed several blue streamers that stunned the sand-eels, the shrimp.

They took a jellyfish to keep. They carried it home in a plastic bot-tle, transferred it to a glass jar and placed it to dry on top of a paper-weight on top of a book on top of the mantelpiece over the stove.

They left behind on the sea peat and rough sand: a mauled sack of Suckie calf nuts, a ruptured colostomy bag, a bleached carton of Her-shey's UHT milk and a solid mass the size of a premature foetus, which they spent a long time trying to identify, turning it over with the toes of their boots, stabbing it with a pointed stick, administering gentle kicks.

It might have been a root, a stone,

a bone.

In their sixth September, out of the gravel on the rock-facing side of the house where almost nothing germinated, a thistle breached and grew to four feet. From the kitchen window, Bell and Sigh caught sight of the thistle. Across the sink and the glass jars soaking on the drain-age rack, ten times a day they mistook it for some kind of small, quiver-ing person,

a child.

They used the huge thistle to prop up the nozzle of the hose. They used the propped nozzle to rinse out the coffee-pot. In dry weather, the scattered grounds dehydrated and blew away. In wet weather, they spread out beneath the gravel and formed a layer.

On calm days, the stagnant air of the low hill smelled like damp hay, like gorse smoke, like a residue of coffee.

Buried beneath the gravel, a metal sediment trap stuffed up with fat of all kinds—olive oil drained from anchovy cans, rapeseed oil scrubbed from frying pans, soured cream and smears of butter. Every pick of waste meagre enough to squeak between the spokes of the plug hole stuck to the congealed fat. This buoyant, alien sludge—part Bell, part Sigh, part dog—agglomerated as gradually and silently as the succulents.

As the loose gutter loosened, its flapping grew louder. As the weather worsened, its flap-rate increased. It battered like a stressed heart.

It didn't wake them.

The house was a ship.

They sailed clean through the worsening nights, drifting on the dead sea of their mattress, limbs retracted beneath the lapping duvet. By then they were deaf to the ship and its wind symphonies; to the full range of its tones—of panic, of taunting, of mirth,

of the sequence that sounded like a wolf whistle, and of the whistle that seemed to end in a question mark.

They could still hear the cow-songs. Gradually they had learned to distinguish a cry of summons from a cry of distress; an exchange of casual reassurance from an appeal of flustered urgency.

They had learned the full cow-scale,

its majors and minors,   its pregnant intervals.

. . .

Every day in September at approximately noon, the farmer walked
up the facing field with a bucket of nuts and the bullocks following,
bellowing. Minutes later he walked down again, the emptied bucket
swinging, the bullocks out of eyeshot, left behind at the trough.

Sometimes he conducted them with a slim stick, with delicate hand
gestures, with only the muscles of his face. Sometimes he made beast-
like noises of rebuke or encouragement:

a bleat, a bark.

If Bell and Sigh met a single cow on the road while they were walking, they turned back. If they saw a parade of free cows in the distance
ahead of them—the farmer in his jeep at the rear, conducting proceedings with his horn—they waited. The farmer kept the herd moving
with short blasts of phrased beeps. He lost his temper in higher, longer,
louder honks.

Bell and Sigh were wary of the unfenced cows. On parade, they
became wilder. Their default impassivity transformed into a drowsy
kind of mischievousness. They became wildebeests—skipping and
bucking,   flicking their tails.

They didn't like to see the farmer too little.

If a few days passed without a sighting, they discussed scenarios
that might likely have prevented their paths from crossing with the
usual regularity: an illness or death in his extended family, a christening
or a wedding, a trip north to sell weanlings.

They didn't like to see the farmer too often.

There were days when, on the morning walk, he passed them four
times, riding in two different vehicles, travelling in both directions.
Each time he shouted a greeting and leaned heavily on his horn, as if,
each time, they were a surprise to him.

. . .

There was so much rain in their sixth autumn that the facing field mustered up a pond. Mallards and grey herons appeared and splashed about, nonchalantly. The pond endured for two days. For two days, it dribbled back down into the field's core. On the third day, reeds were revealed in the rain-logged ground. Bell picked enough to fill a brown glass beer bottle. She singled a stem out from the bunch and split its waxy skin with her thumbnail, scouring the spongy flesh away.

It fell onto the draining board and sprang into a white worm.

There was always,   at least,

one old shopping list crumpled into the cup holder behind the hand-brake between the front seats of the van, accompanied by documentary evidence of the list's expiration: a crumpled supermarket receipt. The lists named only the anomalous items: the things they rarely needed or ran out of, that had already been forgotten once at least before being written down.

Tahini, floss, scrubbers, pumpkin seeds, curry powder, matches, cloves.

Neither Bell nor Sigh ever referred to their lists while shopping. Instead they assumed that the act of writing down the name of a required item was enough to implant it in their shopping-focused minds.

When cups could no longer be supported by the overstuffed holder, one of them would finally throw the paperwork of their old shopping away, along with whatever else came easily to hand—popcorn packets, paper napkins, satsuma peel.

Sigh was always the one who drove; Bell always the one who hopped in and out of the passenger seat to open and close the gate.

It creaked as it swung, discharging drips of rainwater from inside its hollow bars. It nipped her fingers with the steel teeth of its messily welded joints. It tolled a single note

as she slid the bolt.

Them in and the world out.

On one side, there was the incline of compacted gravel, smashed weeds and the marks of skidded tyres. There was the road to every place in the world other than their house.

On the opposite side, their side, there was the overgrown boreen and two thin, parallel paths channelled by the wheels of the van. There was grass stretching up the middle and brambles craning in from either side. There were the crushed plastic pots of herbs past that had eluded their trawler-box, and a few soggy receipts that had missed the mouth of the recycling bin.

From the driver's seat, Sigh would hear the gate's toll: a clank of steel-on-steel that, every time, carried with it the recognition

of how they got to be

all there, all together, at once

for a limited amount of time.

A few years, just,   a few decades, just.

It was inarguably autumn, then.

Together, in the evenings, they still went outside carrying cushions from the Latin sofa and perched on the cleanest stretch of salvaged railway sleeper, flanked by the dogs, encircled by the useless fence, sipping from mugs of sweet, watery whiskey.

They sat facing the mountain. They saw how the grey of rock was fast supplanting the green of fern. They each held its stare. Then the idea reoccurred to them in unison that they might one day, a day of clement weather, climb this particular outcrop.

In spite of the dusk chill and of
                                    how everything was finite—
on the lip of the sleeper, in the lee of the bluff, with the calm of the
whiskey, at the climax of the light, they were together spontaneously
subject to a magnificent peace.

The sycamore had completely disburdened itself. It had filled the
shallow, dinted saucepan of water on the concrete garden path between
gateposts with dead leaves—a portal blocked, its opalescence lost,
    an eye closed,

but as it did, tens more opened scattershot across the facing field.
The bullocks had become less adventurous, by then. Ever since the
pond had come and gone, they had kept to the elevated edges. Only
their hoof-rucks remained in the centre of the surface—each a jagged
pock, glazed with rainwater,   a tapestry of monocles.

                    An eye   an eye
                            an eye
                    an eye   ·   an eye
                            an eye

Chapter Six

The mountain remained, unclimbed,
for the first six years that they lived there.

As a slat of wood fell from the field fence and a wheel came off the
wheelie bin; as a sheet of tin lifted from the cow barn roof and clanked
in the unappeasable wind like a rigid,   useless   wing.
    Inside the roof   the vacant swallow's nest,
               enfeebled by rain,
lost its grip on the spot where it had nestled for six years between in-
tersecting joists and smashed against the concrete floor in an explosion
of moist mud.
    Down the driveway, the robin of the bush finally died. His body was
claimed by a fox who passed in the night; his stretch of hedge was com-
mandeered by a distant cousin.

In the autumn of their seventh year, the thirty-third bottle of washing-up liquid was emptied and thrown away. By then Bell and Sigh had

tested all the different flavours the supermarket had to offer—lemon, apple, power, sunlight—and they had waited, for a week at least at the end of every bottle, for the last syrupy drops to unglue from the base. They had shaken it. They had squeezed it. They had left it to stand, overnight, upside down in a pint glass.

They had done the same for every bottle of honey, of olive oil, of shampoo.

By then the nozzle of the kitchen tap had been broken off and thrown away. In their seventh year, it was accidentally clobbered by the base of the heavy-bottomed pan and clattered down into the sink. The broken end was a jagged-toothed spout until Sigh applied a length of pink shrink tube to soften its edges. The tubing puckered; the water spat.

They called it the Penis Tap.

The original hot-water bottle had been thrown away too. For four months, it had shed red cells from its lining, until—after several hundred too-hot refills and a decisive scalding—its rubber throat split.

Slumped behind the sofa cushions,

it leaked to death.

In six years, essential documents had been renewed approximately six times: tax and insurance discs, bank cards, the standing order that paid the rent, the dog and TV licences, the supermarket loyalty card, the complimentary oil company calendar.

You can't unscramble an egg, the calendars said.

When life hands you lemons, ask for a bottle of tequila.

Footprints in the sand are not made   by   sitting   down.

. . .

Along the bottom edge of every door, thin ropes of hair had formed;
downy cigarillos rolled by the push and swing of come and go. After a
while they detached and wheeled about. They grabbed on to other bottom edges: the rutted rubber of the non-slip bath-mat,
                              the curved beams of the rocking chair.

   Over the years many small objects had been spritzed with Easy Oil.
Creaks and squeaks had been slicked and hushed—the handle of the
back door of the van, the hinges of the garden gate, the padlock of the
shed—but by their seventh autumn, Bell and Sigh rarely used the spray
oil because they were no longer able to hear the smallest noises made
by the aging house: the scheduled cracks, the nocturnal clinking of
pipes, the whisper of the refilling cistern, the chatter of the loose gutter.

   The house's smallest noises seemed to take place inside their bodies, then. Each one was as quiet and as manifest as the pop of a joint;
the grumble of a stomach, the glug of a sinus.

   The inconsistencies that had once kept them awake had, at some
point, become consistent
                         and fallen silent.

They were, finally, no longer able to hear
      the sound of the bullocks at abeyance in the facing field—breathing
heavily, pissing vigorously, calmly shunting—nor the rhythmic clicking
of the electric fence,   nor the songs.
   They were still able to hear
      the unappeasable wind, and how it altered—not only singing, but
enunciating, reciting, imitating.
   The wind was a radio station turned down low,
      a strange car coming up the driveway, an approaching tidal wave,
      and it spoke,   revved   broke.

· · ·

By then   Bell and Sigh had been thoroughly infected by each other's way of speaking. They had each caught the other's inflections and
intonations. They slurred the same pairs of words together and iden-
tically mispronounced others. They skipped the same conjunctions,
maintained the same timbre. By their seventh year, they spoke in a dia-
lect of their own unconscious creation.

They sighed in synchronicity. They hummed the same little non-
sense tunes as they performed the actions that filled the day's shortest
spans of suspended time—the rinsing of a coffee-cup, the tying of shoe-
laces, the approximately seventy seconds it took for a two-mug measure
of cold water to reach boiling point. When they yawned, it was with
identical pronunciation, funnelling the air out to end in an extended
ooooow.

There were times when sentences collapsed,
          words rended into syllables;
                    syllables multiplied and re-coupled.

There were times when they communicated solely by means of ex-
pressive noises. They had mastered each other's mumbles, snorts and
sniffs as they had mastered each other's accents.

It became their commonest form of exchange: basic, yet precise.

Their teeth, untreated, continued to wear down and fissure. Finally
they picked a dental practice in the town, a discoloured white building
with a shiny steel plate screwed to the exterior wall. The seats in the
waiting room appeared to have been salvaged from the smoking car-
riage of a decommissioned train. Each dishevelled magazine was monopolised by photographs of the royal families of foreign countries.

They entered the surgery one by one, and the one who had been left
behind to wait listened through the flimsy door to the din of miniature
drills and hoovers,

    stilted conversation,   the rinse and spit.

They paid together, and as soon as Bell and Sigh had left, the dentist no longer remembered them as two distinct people. Only the lay-
out of the insides of their mouths was clear in his memory: the jagged
edges of a set of central incisors, an overcrowding of premolars, the
presence and absence of wisdom teeth.

The dentist noticed each person's teeth with an intensity that whit-
ened out every other detail. He could not help but experience a crowd

           as a sea   of disembodied mouths and bared grins.

Autumns weaned them   gradually

    off summer, and braced them   gradually

for winter. They were glad to see the ticks die and the tourists leave,
though the volume of visitors seemed to have lessened, as the summers
passed.

Every day as they walked, Bell and Sigh monitored the human
weather.

By their seventh autumn, out along the peninsula, the voices they
overheard were no longer foreign; the bumpers of the cars they met
didn't wear the sticker-plates of separate countries. The holiday homes
either remained unoccupied or appeared to have been re-occupied on a
permanent basis. Sometimes a net curtain parted a crack as they passed;
a light went off or on.

They could not help but feel as if the human seasons had changed.

But the blackberries still came back and festooned the hedges. The fox shit turned to purple and the shit of the blackbirds and thrushes to watery lavender.

Latterly, every left-behind berry wore a fur cap of mould.

Even in late September, they sat out on the cushioned sleeper. Together they insisted—in spite of the cold—in bobble hats and fingerless gloves, grasping hot mugs.

In autumn as it was in spring, the farmer set fires to expunge the undesired gorse. On their sleeper Bell and Sigh sat together in attendance at his spectacle of wind and flame. They watched the smoke and passed a rollie between them, unable to remember, then, which one of them it was who had

originally   smoked.

Though cold and most days damp—in autumn as it was in spring— the landscape was scorched and cadaverous. They sat in the garden to admire its strangeness, together.

Only in the bathroom were they separated.

They were moved by

how quickly a body untidies itself.

Fingernails growing and gobbling up dirt; hair tangling; pores filling with oil and sweat. They showered, and needed to shower again, in just a day or two.

How hard it seemed   to be tidy.

Through their open bedroom window, they listened to the farmer working past midnight; to the thunder of the tractor's engine, the jangle and clap of the trailer.

Was he screaming, they would wonder, his screams drowned out by machine-noise.

They observed the rise and dip of headlamps traversing the bumps in the road. In six years they still had not put up curtains.

The queen spiders, disturbed by the tractor beams, rattled the strands of their webs like silk chains. Across the bedroom ceiling, the disused chains had become wadded up with dust. All night long, in slow motion, they divided into blurred orbs that trembled and fell, like grey stars being born,

burning out, shooting.

The bulb inside the faulty bedside lamp had survived, by then, for over six years. The lamp was a cuboid with a balsa wood frame lined with crepe paper. The paper was embedded with the skeletons of gardenia leaves. The fact that its undersized halogen bulb had never been replaced was as miraculous, to Bell and to Sigh, as the fact that the wood, paper and skeletons had never caught fire.

In the mornings, they found evidence of the farming that happened at night: mud-tracks and patches of bulldozed ditch, a substantial rock knocked out of an ancient wall,

a cigarette butt.

By then the green pelt on the wing mirrors of the van had been joined by a neat row of moss along the seal of each window. A vital mechanism of the handle of the rear door had eroded and snapped, creating the kind of wound that could not be cured by Easy Oil. The only means of opening it was with the aid of the kitchen broom. From a twisted position in the passenger seat, one of them had to shove it handle-first through the grill and prod about until the catch popped.

The broom rode along in the van with them then; relieved of its cupboard-propped life. In the passenger pocket, there was a two-litre bottle of drinking water left over from the summer. Repeatedly, they forgot to remove it.

They were no longer able to hear
its benign, persistent
sloshing.

Voss loved the van even more than his sticks and duvets, his gunge-glazed food dish, his compendium of balls. For Voss, the van repre-sented possibility. As soon as any of its doors opened, even if only for Bell or Sigh to retrieve a cup, a raincoat, the broom, he dashed out of the house and hurdled himself in.

Voss was always ready to go.

He leapt up when the door was only partly open and smacked his skull against its sharp edge. He leapt up even if it wasn't open and his whole, small body bonged against the scratched steel. When they did go out and drive, the longer they drove without stopping—without opening the door to let Voss loose—the louder he would whimper. He whimpered as they slowed for corners or pulled in to pass oncoming vehicles on too-narrow roads. He whimpered whenever he saw a dog already loose in the world and walking. He whimpered out of hope and impatience and envy.

And Pip whimpered too, ill-assured of her own emotions.

All four together, in the aftermath of tremendous excitement,
they arrived at the same places they always went.

. . .

To town for the weekly shop, to the crossroads to put the wheelie bin out, to the joinery to buy sacks of compacted sawdust to burn in the stove. It was cool enough, by autumn, to keep the dogs in the van for a few hours and so they started to make superfluous journeys again. They wound the windows down and Voss rode with his front paws on the passenger dash and Pip, in the back, stood up and laid her chin on the driver's shoulder to catch the gushing breeze.

They found that their beautiful places were no longer blighted by holidaying strangers. There were no cars parked, no snicker of voices. The heather that had once been stamped down by hiking boots had sprung back. Even the sandwich wrappers had disappeared, tuna sweet-corn, chicken stuffing, egg mayonnaise.

Bell and Sigh hopped over stiles and ducked under barbed wires, in silence, treading attentively. They ate their own sandwiches in the van.

There was a ruined tower house with ravens between the battle-ments, a chestnut sapling reaching, arm-like, from the garderobe. There was a dune of sand that collapsed beneath their feet and paws with a snow-like crunch and purity of colour. It was curiously free from shells, pebbles, marram grass. There was a forest on an estuary where they walked a wiggly, uphill loop in relative shelter from the prevailing south-westerlies. They had chosen the path that appeared to be least walked by others. It was too rough and precipitous for brittle-boned old people or intrepid children. It had been ruptured by tree roots. On both sides, an infestation of rhododendrons pushed aside and pressed down the holly and cob-nut and birch, drinking up too much of the sunlight.

There would always be a new place,

or at least   an old place that had

changed.

. . .

Every time they arrived back at the house,
    they were faintly surprised
    to find everything exactly as they'd left it.
    In the sink, a blue-glazed bowl still smeared with the spoon-marks
of white yoghurt. In the kettle, a two-mug measure of tap water. On
the hearthrug, the spoils of a partially chewed stick. Suspended from
the living room curtain rail, a line of monofilament adorned with swiv-
els and crimps, sequins and beads, anchored by a lead pendulum that
moved, gently, stirred by the unpluggable draught,
    the unquenchable breath   of the house.
    Only the smell seemed to change in their absence. Damp dog, in-
cense sticks, boiled greens, mildew and mouldering compost. In their
absence, in the space of a couple of hours, it intensified, becoming
sharp and unpleasant again, becoming   exotic.

Bell and Sigh believed   then
    that the city where they once lived had stayed exactly as it was, as
the house did, every new time they left.
    And so the people they had known had been
                    petrified   by time,
            concentrated   by distance;
that the past was   almost certainly
                                    a model railway.

The light went down. The rain came on. September was carried out on
a week of bad weather.

Indoors they tackled the potted plant situation for the second time in six years. They laid old newspapers down across the oriental rug. Laboriously they uprooted and re-homed the descendants of their first generation of succulents, cacti, geraniums and spider ivies.

At last they were forced to abandon the idea that each pot should be mounted upon a pedestal of some form. There wasn't a square inch of vacant surface left inside the rooms of the house—not the narrow ledges jointing bathtub to wall, not the flat peaks of book heaps, not a sliver of windowsill. They resorted to the floor, plugging the gaps of bare lino between rug islands with the chipped dishes and bowls that cupped the homemade pots. Almost immediately the plants drifted from their allotted spots, encroaching upon the islands themselves.

What once had been empty space was then root, leaf, stem and prickles.

What once had been lifeless floor   undulated.

October mornings peeled the night cloud back to its subcutaneous lilac tissue.

The leaves earned their name by leaving the trees. Browned and blistered foliage cascaded from the sycamore, swilling into the exterior nooks of the house, ruffling the gravel, snagging on the tortured remains of the thistle, bottlenecking and compacting in the corner where the wheelie bin was kept, so that when it was taken off for collection, its absence created a rectangular hollow the shape of a short, stocky pillar

that held its shape   for several seconds

before

crumbling.

. . .

Late in the autumn, they pegged out their dank wool on the washing-line for the southwesterlies to slap dry in preparation for winter. They pulled down the scarves from the bedroom curtain rail and whipped them against the concrete path. They brushed off spent cocoons and dust-logged webs; they banished the moths
and torpid wasps.

They were glad that they could wear wool again—jumpers, cardigans, scarves. These were the shapeless, timeless garments in which they felt most comfortable.

They tried to buy the right vegetables and fruit for the season they were in: conference pears and red cabbage, a squash whose taut segments of peel they arranged into a pale corona around a circular slice of sun-coloured flesh on the mottled black countertop.

By their seventh year, they had succeeded in eating the nettles.

They had eaten the sea spinach too, the wild garlic and thyme and mint, even the dandelions.

Two bullocks pressed their foreheads together and pushed one another, half-heartedly, around the facing field.

When the farmer came, every autumn, with his livestock trailer and took them away, two by two, Bell or Sigh turned up the volume of the radio to drown out the clatter of steel, the clamour of confused moo-ing, and then, the following spring, they pretended it was the same herd that came back again. They reassured one another that each new bullock was not new but simply returned from its winter confinement, two by two—

black and white, white and black.

In the facing field all winter, the bullocks' neglected possessions shifted, switching position, uncertainly following one another. There was a tattered sack of feed, an upturned bucket, a tuft of coarse tail hair.

There were the gulls and crows—

black and white, white and black.

And cow pellets,

strewn along the road. At first dry and hard. Then bloated with rain. Finally a fibrous mush, daubed across the crude tarmac.

Voss sucked up the pellets as they passed, or bit the crusty skin off a set pat, revealing its creamy filling. Pip hung back for every promising scent. She folded her right front leg down and rolled her neck, calculatedly, into a segment of fox shit. She painted a purple-black stroke across her fur so that once they had arrived home again, Bell or Sigh would have to rope her lead around the pipe of the outside tap and fetch the rubber glove, the rancid cloth, the bottle of puppy shampoo.

They each tried to be the one who reached the tap first; who took responsibility for the grisly job of hosing down the disgraced dog. They each rushed to be first,

and spare the other.

They walked the way they always walked. They passed the same pair of classically patterned donkeys. The donkeys greyed, as if fading away in patches, until one day in their seventh autumn, Bell and Sigh approached the field to find it deserted. They idled at the wall holding a bag that contained a turnip chopped into blocks. The next evening there were still no donkeys and so they carried the turnip around the peninsula and home, in the deep pockets of their raincoats, bouncing against their hips.

There were no donkeys the next evening either, or the next,
as if the field had finally osmosed them.

And the blocks lay in their bag on a corner of the kitchen counter-top for several days,

turning stiff,   turning tough,

turning to yellow leather.

In Octobers the last mackerel, the last blackberry, the last thrift, the last summer bird,

but the first winter bird,   the first puffball;

the pink of a cold grey cloud refracted in a cold grey puddle.

Every day they walked the way they always walked and lit the fire at the moment they arrived home and felt warm as soon as the cold glass glowed. That was the only prompt they needed—a certain quality of light in a certain shape—to be warmed.

In their seventh year, the crack in the glass of the stove door that had for eighteen months remained no longer than a crayon suddenly started to advance in both directions, to creep a little further with every soft tap. It was the length of a pencil, the length of a ruler. Then it dis-severed into a crevasse,

a lopsided wink in their nightly glow,   a jagged-toothed grin.

They walked the way they always walked: down the hill road to the beach, on around the peninsula. The heath reddened, the snipe re-turned. There was a gorse bush that looked like a gigantic tumbleweed,

a gorse bush that looked like a pouncing lynx,
a gorse bush that looked like a mushroom cloud.

There were shags between the herring gulls, oystercatchers in a gag-
gle on the rocks. And they called them oysterpipers, even though they
knew it was wrong.

There was a tangled, salt-scrubbed, noodle-like stick that Pip and
Voss yanked between them in a vicious tug-of-war, until it snapped and
each dog stumbled back and ran off in opposite directions with their
respective portion of stick, respectively triumphant.

There were grey seals at rest between the juts and cusps beneath
the undercut cliff path wailing notes too long and low for any sea-
bird. In storms the seal mothers towed their calves through the co-
agulated froth, nudging them onto reefs and pebbly strands safe from
the toss and thrash, the monstrous, contrary momentum of the under-
sea because   they had not yet learned

how to steady and moor themselves;
how to breathe using only the oxygen stored
in their muscles and blood.

They listened to the weather forecast, once every hour. They compared the meteorologist's reports with the views from their windows,
or stood out on the welcome mat with their chins tilted skywards, or
the pad of a licked finger lifted to the wind. They levelled their binoculars at the horizon.

When gales were forecast, they cleared the washing-line of remnants, locked the wheelie bin into the shed and tucked the van into its
nook. They tidied the potted herb garden into the trawler-box along
with the hose-pipe, the rancid cloth, the puppy shampoo. They tied

down the loose things and rounded up the untied things. They filled
the bathtub with water.

They always forgot about the BEWARE OF DOG sign, all the way
down at the end of the driveway, out of sight. By their seventh October, they had reached their fourth sign. It hung from the steel bars surrounded by the rusted staples and sun-bleached cable ties of signs past,
dinging softly.

Storms tugged at the clanking sheet of tin on the cow barn roof, in-
crementally peeling it back, like a sardine can. Storms cut further into
the undercut cliff edge out of the peninsula, slashing down the ferns,
brandishing and burnishing the ungrowing grass. Storms unstrung the
power lines and whipped them about, chasing off the ducks and parting
the killed-back undergrowth such that chasms of grey bedrock peeked
through, narrow patches of the landscape's pale scalp.

The view from their windows showed the low hill in fast-forward
mode. Nothing stayed still, not a single chip of gravel or length of gutter or lopsided fence-post, not even the trunk of the scruffy spruce,

nothing,

except the mountain.

Storms brought lightning and thunder.

Indoors they counted the seconds between flashes and claps. They
guessed which was highest: the roof, the tree, the telegraph pole.

Storms clung to storms.

A trampoline appeared at the far side of the facing field, and rested,
legs in the air,

until being moved along by the next storm.

. . .

Storms broke off new pieces of the house, spiting their efforts—the lid of the kitchen extractor fan, an ancient telephone wire, several more slates. They were smashed, or swept from sight, or retrieved and condemned to the graveyard of utensils on the top of the fridge.

In the aftermath of the storms, the landlord came with his ladder to stick the broken-off pieces back onto his house again. He brought new clips and re-affixed the phone wire. He nailed the un-smashed slates back into place. He heaped the roof of the cow barn with jute sacks of quarried sand.

The sand sacks sat—both pert and slumped. They formed a strange, bumpy horizon such that it seemed almost as if the slaughtered bullocks had come back, and climbed up there, and lain down

again   together.

They sat.

In the overlong evenings, in a circle of the leavings of their half-finished activities. With the stove glass glowing and grinning,

the potted plants erupting and spilling,

they sat. In the overlong evenings,

eating their dinners in seven-day cycles.

They had, by then, substituted rapeseed oil for olive, coarse sea salt for Himalayan pink, stone-ground wholegrain flour for white spelt. They had developed a taste for Chinese Five Spice and discovered a more efficient way of slicing onions. But the essential foundations of each dinner remained unaltered. In six years they had never once been brave enough to attempt cooking something entirely new and run the risk of having to eat a horrible dinner.

They sat.

In the overlong evenings, in which dinner was everything, battling against the catastrophic reception of their elderly television set. It showed a blizzard of static with shadowy figures shifting beneath, stammering unfinished sentences, disseminating into specks

of   scattered   ash.

NO SIGNAL, the screen declared with perfect clarity, and died.

Then they brought out the laptop and the discs in their cardboard slip-cases that had come free with a Sunday broadsheet years ago; a newspaper they had bought solely for its free offer for eight long weeks. They wiped the discs on their trouser legs and blew softly into the drive.

Then they watched

The Blue Planet,

afresh.

The clock in the van had never been right. None of the nearby buttons seemed to control it and neither of them, in seven years, had felt compelled to consult the user manual. Once a year, for half a year, the hour of the van fell into step with real time, though the minutes never made sense.

As there was van time, so there was kitchen time: a radio alarm clock on the shelf of coffee-pots above the socket switch. This was the clock to which they cooked. If it happened to stop, everything would dry up;   everything would burn.

During storms the electricity often dipped and the kitchen clock stopped for a second and came back. Its red digits blinked at midnight and they each rushed to spare the other the drudgery of resetting it, which involved the repetitive prodding of a single button—the patience

of running through every minute of every hour between midnight and
the time it happened to be,   a cascade that made time seem
                        so brittle, so hollow.
And then they always came up a little short,   a little over.

Good days were rare then, in Octobers, and so at the end of every one,
they remarked upon how good it was. They reassured each other.
    That was a good day, they said. That was a good day.

They had checked their email accounts, for a while.
    In the beginning, they might have met a week's worth of missed
messages at once. But as time passed, a week yielded no messages at all,
then a month, a year—only the tiny, white hand with its index finger
lifted, as if checking the wind direction.
    They forgot their passwords,
    as they had forgotten the numbers of their old bus routes, and the
numbers of their old houses and old streets, and the names of the old
pubs where they used to meet,   and of their old
                                        friends.

On the internet, they checked the marine atlas. After dark on the days
they had taken trips, they retraced their daylight routes. On virtual
road maps, on the Latin sofa, they turned down the tracks that had,
hours earlier, appeared to be driveways. They peered over the trees
that had obscured their view. They verified what they had found and
compared it with the recent past when the internet footage had been

recorded. They assimilated the change of season, the advance or clearance of undergrowth, the fragmented appearances of bystanders.

They travelled a twenty-mile radius from the house, never straying a yard further, in the past or present, online or in life.

In Octobers their side of the mountain turned russet, one level up from the charred gorse, one level down from the rock.

At first they could never remember the source of the russet colour. Then they brought out the binoculars and identified it as the dying bracken. Each leaf, at maximum focus, was made up of several perpendicular strands either side of the stem. Each strand was a faultless miniature of the leaf as a whole.

They remembered how, after having scrabbled up beyond the reach of the gorse fires, the ferns only died back anyway.

By then   the embroidered cushion covers were in shreds.

Their sequins, beads and coin-sized mirrors had fallen off. Their loose, matted threads draggled from the sofa like the cobwebs that draggled from the ceiling crooks.

Before they went upstairs to bed, together Bell and Sigh fixed the mess of mangled textiles that concealed the nakedness of the Latin sofa. Along with the sequins, beads and mirrors, there was always a selection of detritus from whatever dinner they happened to have eaten that night:

a grain of rice, a particle of the crackling of a roasted spud,

a broccoli bud.

They straightened the throw blanket. They lined up the cushions and swept the crumbs away.

And yet, they left their bed undressed.

During the day items of clothing lay on the disordered duvet like small mammals curled up in sleep. Pip stole the socks that fell to earth. She liked the balled-up ones especially. She shook them out to their full extension and swung them around. She thumped the duvet, and ran away.

There were juvenile potted plants that did not grow in the same shape or shade of green as their progenitors. They put on new colours; they threw down new shadows. They survived, sometimes for weeks on end, by suckling the steam that rose from the saucepans, and from damp clothes crammed onto warm radiators. The same steam steeped into every porous surface of the house, the papers and wools, the grout between tiles.

It subdued their interiors, at first,   and then the rot set in.

White sheets bound around footballs in the branches of the beech trees outside the primary school they passed on the way into town; each that was not already tangled, thrashing.

On the last weekend of their seventh October,
                    they missed the changing of the clocks.

It took them three days to realise their mistake. It was the angelus that did it. Then they made a decision to continue as they were—to preserve the summer, sleeping on through the dark mornings in exchange for an extra hour of brightness in the evenings.

They decided to create a time zone unique to the house.

. . .

Walking around the peninsula at dusk, they saw the lighthouse five miles south across the Atlantic, out on its islet. In summer it was an illusory bump, but every evening from October on, it pinpointed itself with a flashing beam. It glinted at the moment they turned back up the hill again, dependably.

A salute,

    a conspiratorial wink,

        a warning.

They were moved by: how quickly the house untidied itself.

They tidied up, despondently. Their low standards stretched only to the emptying of bins, the laundering of sheets and wiping down of countertops, a cursory sweep of the kitchen lino.

There was a mustard-coloured scuff in the cream paint that ran right to the top of the staircase, and on the highest step, several coffee-coloured drips.

There were coffee drips elsewhere—on the white wood boards and the lower half of walls and doors—as if they danced with their brimming cups every morning, quick-stepping, spinning around.

There was a bottomless supply of hair that flowed from the dogs, and dust from the ash that flowed from the fire, and they had combined—the dog hair and ash dust—into a new kind of matter, sticky, quilted.

There was the bathroom ceiling mildew. Each winter it rose back through the most recent layer of brilliant white—tiny circles, dark but dull, one by one pronouncing themselves from corner to corner, crook to crook.

They put out the sweepings of their years.

They waited until after dark. And stood in the wind of the low hill. They slashed open the glutted hoover bags and emptied them into the tempests.

Overhead, on clear nights, stars cluttered the sky like punctures in the blackness   like opened eyes.

Out on the low hill after dark, it felt as if it might be possible to take out a switchblade,   reach up   and stab out

a new eye

a new eye

a new eye

a new eye

a new eye

a new eye

a new eye

a new eye

a new eye

a new eye

a new eye

a new eye

a new eye

a new eye

a new eye

a new eye

a new eye

a new eye

a new eye

a new eye

a new eye

a new eye

Chapter Seven

The mountain remained, unclimbed,
for the first seven years that they lived there.

As the timber planks of the garden bench rotted, warped and snapped.

As the motor of the handheld blender coughed, choked and sputtered out.

As the crack in the stove door expanded and divided into tributaries.

As new small objects were lost between the splits of the bedroom floorboards—a hair tie, a staple, the plastic barb of a clothes tag.

As new items of clothing were neglected and stacked up on the bedroom chair—a laddered vest, a bobbled jumper, a vagrant glove.

As the flies that had been killed in summer by the sole of the slipper and glued by their guts to the bedroom walls built up, and grew old, their slack legs waving daintily in the through breeze.

Still   they had not climbed the mountain.

As the power button of the shower unit broke off, and so they pressed the plastic kernel instead, hoping they would not be electrocuted.

. . .

By then   all of their clothes were jumbled together,
                                        .   as was their stationery.
     Pencils of every grade, distributed between vessels and rooms, once
arranged according to logic, were incoherently mingled, disunited and
reunited, their leads broken or blunted, their butts chewed.
     By then   their once-new fillings had discoloured to precisely
the same shade as their discoloured teeth.
     Their hair had progressively greyed. The skin of their faces had
progressively crinkled in accordance with the sides of their bodies they
were most likely to sleep on—to crush, ruthlessly, into the pleats of the
pillow all night.
     Still   they had not climbed the mountain.

The kitchen kickboards were increasingly toe-scuffed;
     the hood of the cooker increasingly freckled with grease.
The kitchen clock had started to malfunction; it played the radio very
quietly and refused to be switched off. No matter how fiercely they
clicked the dial, the whisper of informative voices rose from its speak-
ers, an impromptu song.
     The outline of their most-used wooden spoon had been abraded to
a smoother, sleeker version of itself. The garlic press had been lost but
for the stainless-steel hole-pocked insert through which they would
hammer small, peeled cloves with the handle of a lesser-used spoon.
     By then   dozens of dish-scourers had been expended—their
sponge bodies wizened, their wiry faces matted and fried by the resid-
ual heat of the hobs.
     And still   they had not climbed the mountain.

. . .

The years that it remained unclimbed piled up around them like their old clothes.

They had intended to put up a shower curtain, a bookshelf, a couple of coat hooks.

They had intended to frame paintings, to replace the battery in the smoke alarm, to have the boiler serviced, to plant some hard-wearing shrubs along the garden wall—

hydrangea, spiraea, rose.

In their eighth winter, the clanking sheet of tin on the cow barn roof finally levered itself to freedom. It was severed by a strong southwesterly and swooped, like a tin buzzard, across the stretch of gravel that separated the shed from the house. It crash-landed against the gable, faintly scarring the unpainted plaster,

a rust-red graze through the rhinoceros grey.

For seven years they had carelessly pegged cloths and socks to the wire mesh of the garden fence. In their eighth winter it buckled, and then the landlord came with a cordless strimmer to assault the overlong lawn. As he worked he sliced several holes through the intact bottom end of the mesh by mistake. After he had finished, the dogs could duck under the buckled fence even more easily than they could jump over it.

But they didn't.

They just stood on the grass as they had always done, with their wet noses raised to the wind and their whiskery cheeks chuffing.

In seven years they had not once chosen to escape.

At certain stages of the cold months in which they did not swim, the sensation of being immersed and its attendant vulnerability would re-

turn to them in other forms. The motion of speeding along a straight
road brought it back, or being buffeted by storm-force gales, or calmly
enfolded by drunkenness.

By then   they would put voices to the birds as they put voices to
the dogs as they put voices even to inanimate things. They translated
calls and songs, yips and whines into words and phrases. They translated the thuds and clicks,

creaks and ticks—

speaking up, speaking back   on behalf of the house.

Every evening they walked the way they always walked. Every evening they pointed out to each other, and repeated, the small changes
since their last walk, a full day ago. A piece of litter in winter was a
bright flash against the drab—a lustrous, silvered, fluorescent scrap—
the inside-out wrapper of a chocolate bar, the buckled can of an energy
drink, a squashed bottle of pure mineral water still full and floating in
an impure stream, the rigid triangular package of a turkey stuffing sandwich—it lay upside down in the ditch like a tiny, pointed mountain.

There was half a satsuma, unpeeled, that had travelled intact
through a fox's intestines. There was a turd pecked to pieces by a magpie's exacting beak, and a pink cloth submerged in a brown puddle like
a piece of cold meat.

There was a black-wrapped bale plonked in a gateway, and plastic strips garlanding posts and briars, caught on the barbs of the wire
fences and the needles of the scruffy spruce pines;

thinned and tenderised by time,

rustling like tassels,

dangling from the prongs of the roadside hawthorns,

as if the blackbirds had hung out their frazzled wings.

. . .

The dogs stalked the tassels, convinced, from a distance, that they were tiny, fluttering cats.

In seven years a handful of wild creatures had been violently murdered along the route of their evening walk. There had been a wood mouse plucked from under a fern and nibbled to death in a fuss of muffled squealing. There had been an unresponsive frog on the mudbank of a ditch puddle that they humanely dispatched with the fast whack of a rock. There had been a kit rabbit that the dogs wrenched between them for a protracted moment—one latched to the rear, one to the ears.

The sound made by the racking apart of its skeletal system was the twisting of a stiffened lid. It climaxed with a pop of release. Ravelled intestines unravelled and gushed out through the lacerated skin of the kit's stomach, sploshing onto the knobbled tarmac. Pip won the front legs, shoulders and head. Voss won the larger, softer share, and they both tried to swallow as much and as quickly as they could before the rabbit in its gory parts was wrestled away from them and thrust over the hedge.

They all arrived home spattered with blood.

They walked in fog, in rain, in wind. They walked when they could see nothing but the white miasma surrounding them; when the road-wide puddles had reached their full, man-sized expanse; when the electricity wires sagged and wailed and struggled to stay fastened to their poles.

They walked all the way to Ulaanbaatar, without leaving their road.

They thought they were taking the dogs out; the dogs thought they were taking them out.

Any small change in routine would have been catastrophic.

Their catastrophes were featherweight,   then.

A square of chocolate that refused to break evenly along its given line. A preferred brand of yoghurt that had gone out of stock. A strand of fluff against an eyeball that they could feel but not seem to pluck off.

They didn't go for long drives in the van any more.

By then   they had realised that everything they needed was within a mile or two of the house. And so they made their long journeys on the internet.

On the internet, they could fly.

They could dive without any of the equipment.

They could travel back in time.

They sat in the van on the driveway, passing the binoculars between them, watching for the pigeons and crows, the rat that lived under the shed, the goat that lived up the mountain.

Every winter they bought a bottle of washing-up liquid with a festive theme: winter berries,

                        pine fresh,

                                    clementine spice.

Through their broken television set late at night came the ads for latte makers and compilation albums, a living room disco ball, an eight-in-one torch, scissors capable of transforming courgettes into spaghetti and a special mangle for the sundering apart of apples.

Just like a regular mangle, they said, only twenty quid dearer.

By then   their original collection of kitchen equipment had
suffered a significant quantity of injury and loss. Where once there had
been wine glasses, there were only mugs. Where once there had been a
surplus of teaspoons, there was a dearth. Where once there had been a
full set of dinner-plates, there was only one.

Where once there had been a percolating coffee-pot, there was only
a portentous stain on the ceiling above the cooker—the brown mark
left behind by its explosion, surrounded by a wobbly circle of dimmer
splashes.

The coffee stain loomed, stratus-like, over everything they withdrew
from the weakening oven: a defrosted loaf of bread, a tray of roasted
nuts, a dish of winter fish—the white of a ling's skinned sides, the scar-
let of cherry tomatoes, the charred green of thyme and rosemary twigs,
a gold pond of oil—and five baked rooster potatoes, the slit cut into
their skins puffed into a white seam between squeezed pink lids.

During the overlong evenings, they played Connect 4.

Their set was missing several of the yellow counters and two of the
reds. When they first started playing, the absent counters made no difference, but as they practiced and improved, the games started to drag
on and exhaust the supply of the set's parts, and so they cut duplicate
counters out of thick card, painted them yellow and red, but still there
came a point at which no game could ever be finished; at which they
were both able to foresee every coming move. The blue board, standing erect, would fill up until there wasn't a single slot left empty, even
though neither of them had won.

. . .

They talked in bed,   lying face up, unable to discern anything
but semblances through the moonless dark.

    They talked in bed,   making comparisons with their
earlier lives, until all that they ever made comparisons with were earlier
versions of their shared life,   there.

    They talked in bed,   in the dialect of the house, re-
citing the day's final litany of thoughts aloud. They stopped in unison,
never tapering off, never saying goodnight,

    but simultaneously reaching a mutual end,

                  and falling asleep.

There was the pale blue of the bed-sheet and the slightly different pale
blue of the duvet cover and the slightly different pale blue of the rumpled winter morning sky. On the floor between the bed and the bedroom window, there was the stinking duvet and the sleeping dogs in a
grotto of their sea-salvaged belongings:

    the chewed foam of a flip-flop, a toilet ballcock,

                  a knotted sock.

They talked in bed,   wondering aloud
whether there was a chance   there might have been
some kind of   magnificent   occurrence,
    the force of which they had failed to fully appreciate.
They had noticed: an atmosphere, a whiff of bleach. When
they passed the pub on the way to the supermarket, it looked as if it
was shuttered and locked, and in the supermarket, it seemed as if the
other people had   perhaps   started to avoid them

                  too.

It had become difficult to buy canned chickpeas, flour, cartons of passata, toilet roll.

The smallest of their toes and fingers turned red and bent in weather that was mostly cold but fluctuating. Inside their poorly heated rooms, their extremities itched and swelled until the dried skin blistered.

The number of house spiders had dwindled, but the family of house mice had grown. They cavorted beneath the floorboards at night and pooed along the spines of the upstanding books. They ate mouse-sized holes in loaves of bread left out overnight on the kitchen countertop. They stole strips of brown paper bags from the recycling bucket and shredded them into mattresses. They plotted out passageways beneath the shelter of the potted plants. Nothing was flowering, then. Instead the spider ivies coiled their tentacles around every protuberance. They softly clinched the trinkets and seashells and preserved reptiles, obscuring the unlabelled brown boxes with their top flaps taped shut, the cigarillos of fur, the multifunctional fruit bowl.

Where once there had been fruit, there was a conch shell, a cauliflower, a ping-pong ball.

What once had been room,

then was mousery,

orangery,

insectarium.

They forgot, on a regular basis, where the plug for the kitchen sink was kept, and the numerical passwords for their internet banking. They remembered, on a regular basis, a scene or prop or sensation from years ago. A memory would occur with no clear distinction as to whether it

rose directly from an experience of their own or had been recalled indi-
rectly from the account of something experienced by the other.

One of them had once broken a nose;

worn an orthodontic retainer;

owned a poster of Kurt Cobain pointing a gun into the camera;

seen a kingfisher.

Together they could picture the speckles on its iridescent wings, the
tilt of its bayonet beak. Together they could remember a rowboat bob-
bing on a calm lake; the slant of the seats as a plane ascended, the jar-
ring bump as it landed again—a flight gate (A23) and a window seat
(23A) down the side of which an entire pencil-case was inexplicably
lost. And the sway of a Ferris wheel, the clop of a pony circling a cir-
cus ring, an embarrassing sex scene, a pike that got away, the skin of
the back of a child's neck on a bus—white and thin as tissue—and an
old man in a train station with an overflowing suitcase thrown open on
the ground in front of him. He had been kneeling in a circle of spilled
plastic bags, string, a dozen small packages swaddled in re-used tinfoil.
There had been a security guard looming over the old man with an ex-
pression that was part annoyance, part pity.

Together they remembered: a baby niece, a brother who did a para-
chute jump, a great-aunt who died of a brain tumour, though it was, by
then, impossible to remember

whose baby niece,

whose brother,

whose great-aunt.

They filled hours.

They found there were so many hours in a life,

and two hooded crows on the same telegraph pole at the same time

every morning, and linnets, and meadow pipits. The reed buntings had
gone back up the mountain. The wheatears had continued on to Iberia
and North Africa.

They watched the rain
feeding the empty fields. Run-off and spring water gushed down the
unclimbed mountain in numberless rivulets, pooling in the tough and
treeless ground, until the fields broke out in ducks again, in gulls and
grey herons.

They watched the rain
and though it did not rain constantly, it never stopped for long enough
that the low hill dried out. The puddles rose and fell. The ink clouds
gathered together and pulled apart in a winter-long cycle of threat and
reprieve.

In the dark, it sounded like a crackling fire.

They went out and walked as soon as the rain stopped, and it always started again at the moment they reached the tip of the peninsula,
the point of their walk furthest from the house. They charged back
through the showers, sheets and torrents, with the gales blowing their
hoods down; with the rain sluicing off the tails of their coats and satu-
rating the thighs of their trousers; with their runners squelching. The
drenched dogs insisted upon stopping in order to shake, jingling their
shackles in a volley of angry drops.

They watched the rain
and in their peripheral vision, the hedges floated and sank. On every
rung of every bar of every gate,

                              a drip.

They watched the rain
staining the windowless, road-facing gable of the house a dark-
ened shade of mustard grey, as if the unpainted plaster had suddenly
scowled. They watched to see if their road would flood and if the

floodwater would render their only exit route impassable; to see if they would soon

no longer be able to get

to the places they had no cause to go.

New storms, called Ewan, Brian, Ophelia.

New fog arrived with the calm that followed, as thick and impurely white as cream. It poured into the landscape, clotting up and blotting out the panorama, pocket by pocket. They raised their hands and patted the pillowy air, demonstrating its softness.

In November, the first frosts.

Algae, like brown frogspawn, ballooned up through the tarmac and moss and barely still-alive grass blades along the middle of the road. They would walk at sunset, with the winter moon and the winter sun— identical fog-smothered orbs—standing together in the sky on opposite sides of the peninsula, facing each other down. When the sun was low and peeking and the tide low too, the rock-pools would burn,

their salt water clenching the light,

curdling amber,   violet,   peach.

Ewan, Brian and Ophelia shook new props down from the sky, and threw them up from the bottom of the sea and cleaved them off the underside of the cliff and lobbed them onto the path: gannet crap and clods of grass-capped mud, a strip of synthetic cork that Pip tossed and chased like a baton, a brittle-star they carried home and laid out on the mantelpiece above the stove.

They slept perfectly, every freezing night. They dreamed often of dogs plummeting from cliffs,

though not always their dogs,

their cliffs.

. . .

In November the song of the house was a gurgling in the throat of the bathroom tap, a crackling emitted by the tangled TV cables. The boiler growled. The fridge purred. The radiators burbled. A load of heavy, wet wool slopped around in the metal drum of the washing machine. It reached the end of its cycle and the control panel beeped, indignantly.

They couldn't hear any of it.

First thing every winter morning, the rectangular top pane of the bathroom window held no wild roses or fuchsia, only their drab, crooked skeletons and a mosaic of bald patches where the field and light wept through.

In the centre of the ceiling, the dwindling bulb flickered inside its frosted dome like a clouded moon.

The letterbox, though still weighted down with the original rock, was no longer a biscuit tin. The tin had been replaced by a container of watertight Tupperware. Capacious as a basin; larger than the largest package they had ever received. It did not rust.

The time-telling digits of the clock in the van no longer came on as the key was twisted in the ignition. Instead they warmed up in accordance with the engine, red against the blank black, slowly becoming inflamed.

Still they relied on the free calendar supplied yearly by the oil company.

Complete self-control, it said, *is eating one salted peanut.*

Accept that some days you are the pigeon, and some days you are the statue.

When nothing goes right,   go left.

. . .

Frost attacked the potted herb garden. It sapped the tender, flavour-some leaves, reducing the mint to twigs, starving the weeds and pruning back the shrubbery.

Ice was rare,

but the illusion of ice was everywhere—
there was the hail on the surface of the puddles. There was a floating swatch of woven polypropylene coal sack. There was the way the light limply touched the wet tarmac.

They did not slip.

In terrible weather they would go to the wood on the estuary for their evening walk, for the paltry shelter provided by its mixed canopy. Even the irrepressible rhododendrons were in death mode then. The weakest trees had been pitched off the edges of the banks by storms; their crowns drowned in the murky water, their roots leaving wide, collapsing gaps in the path, as if they were still gripping on with the tips of their toe bones,

trying to heave themselves back up.

There would be shelducks in the shallows then, a solitary greenshank. From the highest point of the wood, the tallest, barest branches formed a roof and tinged the view the colour of thin wine,

a purple brume beneath the wiggly lines of rain.

Many reusable shopping bags—of canvas, jute and hessian, of recycled plastic bottles, tyres and string—had been hung on the hooks on the back of the kitchen door, so many that, by then, it would only open wide enough to admit a single body at a time.

They would queue to enter the kitchen from the living room, the living room from the kitchen.

Every item of food, with the exception of their own potatoes, had been carried into the house in one of the reusable bags, mostly the several closest to the front. The layer of bags at the very back, squashed against the timber of the door, remained untouched. There was still a flake of the skin of a red onion inside one, some dry earth inside another, a few strands of hair from an ear of corn.

There was still the occasional sun patch, through one or other of the windows of the house. Voss was always the first to locate it.

He shifted as it shifted;   it kindled the grey in his coat.

In their eighth December, they finally bought a potted Christmas tree. There were only three left in the deserted garden centre. They got down on their knees to examine the condition of each diminutive fir. They studiously chose the worst, the one that seemed least likely to be chosen by others.

Its trunk leaned, the lowest branches were bare, and it had no smell, no matter how much they crushed its needles between their fingertips. In the house, it took them a long time to clear a space. At last they mounted the pot on an upturned crate between the television and the stove. They covered the crate in Christmas paper. They wound a string of multicoloured lights around and around the wonky tree.

Rain turned to ice.

Hail collected in the ditches and remained, unmelted, all night.

In their eighth December, for the first time, it snowed.

Their first snow was dry as plain flour, but with the gloss of jam sugar. It fell for hours without pause. It moved heavily and lazily, at first. Later the wind picked up and the sluggish squalls became nimble blizzards, hurrying over open ground, colliding with hedges and dumping their loads. And the dumped snow built gradually into ridges and mounds,   into mountain ranges.

In the morning, dog piss in the stainless snow.

They found their well had frozen in the night, and trudged to the farmer's house carrying as many empty bottles and cartons as could be retrieved from the recycling bin. They were relieved to find he had a deeper well that was still flowing, and to meet his father, who did not seem so stooped in the armchair where he sat in the kitchen, beside the log stove. He was reading the obituaries. They took up two and three pages now, the farmer told them. Every kind of sport had been called off and the processors wouldn't take all the milk his cows had to give. He was pouring it down the drain, he said. Now his soak-aways were clogged with ice cream. He stood well back as they took it in turns to lean over his tap.

At home again they made coffee. They lit the fire and filled a bucket with snow and placed it on the warm dais with the broken door of the stove swung open. They were surprised by what little water it amounted to. They were disappointed by the several hours that had to pass before their bucket of solid became less than a jug of liquid. And so they cooked the snow instead, in the deepest saucepan on the largest hob, stirring it with a wooden paddle they'd never used before, that had come free with a bag of porridge years previously. In the bottom of the saucepan after it had melted

there was a sediment of grit,

even though   the snow they had started with

                    had appeared to be   immaculate.

Finally they poured it down the toilet. They stood on the tips of their toes and stretched their arms up, trying to generate the force of a flush by means of altitude and speed.

They were pleased   about   the cancelled sport.

Snow, they found, emitted its own strange light: a cold but simmering phosphorescence.

For the four nights it remained, there was no pure dark. Instead the facing field glowed like a grounded moon. Through the frosted glass of the lower, larger pane of the bathroom window, the familiar soft-focused shapes of the driveway were replaced by a formless blaze of white.

By the fifth morning of their first snow, they had eaten all the fresh food in the fridge, all the tinned fish and butterbeans in the cupboard, even the dregs of a packet of dried, faded split peas.

On the fifth morning, it showed signs of abating. No new snow fell and the sitting snow started to thin   and give
                                        and separate,
        to turn clear, to turn to water,
    and then the ditch streams   rose, gushed, spat,
and the landmarks that had been concealed were revealed again, their colours replenished—the cat-shaped rock, the jagged fence-post, the gap and the smudge—and new landmarks were delineated by the disappearing snow—the porcelain bowl of a toilet buried in a patch of frost-stripped scrub,
    a lump of silage, a dislodged boulder.
The mounds and ridges lasted longest, banked-up in the lees of the hedges. From the point of view of the mountain, it seemed as if fat chalk lines had been drawn around the perimeter of each field.

. . .

The snow stirred up the low hill's smallest particles.

Fibres were manipulated, pulled apart, pulped together and compressed   like corned beef.

The year laid down another fabric. The tree traced out another ring.

They made a wreath from lengths of yew and fixed it to the field-facing
door like a feathered port-light,   a giant spy-hole.

Their landlord called to the house every Christmas Eve with a box
of Cadbury Roses and a sack of coal, and they reciprocated with a bottle of wine and a biscuit assortment. They asked permission to stay for
another year, to continue to live   exactly as they lived
in the house,   his house,   their house.

For the farmer they bought a litre of whiskey. He didn't put up a
wreath, but there was a single, tall candle in the most prominent of his
front windows. At Christmas he was calving, and so they followed the
glare of the small shed adjacent to the parlour, and he stepped out to
greet them in a rubber apron. He repeated, every year, as he wiped his
hands, that they really shouldn't have brought anything.

But you are our breakdown assist, they said. Our home alarm system, our ambulance, our bus.

Behind him in the doorway of the small shed in a halo of artificial
light, there was a blood-slicked newborn in a nest of hay, lifting its lax
neck, its elastic lips held in the shape of a bawl they could not hear.

Without their original families to direct proceedings, they felt, every
Christmas Day, mildly bewildered.

They were post-family then,

post-doctrine,

post-consumerism.

And they had left themselves with nothing to celebrate.

Their eighth Christmas morning was windy and wet. Beneath the elevated potted tree in its dress of lights, there was a ring of newspaper-wrapped packages: an antler for Pip and a squeak-ball for Voss, a bottle of port and a packet of salted macadamia nuts, a cluster of figurines from the charity shops,   socks,   and a poinsettia.

The figurines were a porcelain fawn, a pig in a bowler hat, a Child of Prague.

They celebrated anyway.

They drove to the peninsula, parked, and sat in the back of the van with the seats flipped down, cross-legged on a rag-rug around the camping cooker. They tended a pot of lentil soup, putting out brown bread and smoked salmon, cups and spoons until the pot started to spit and the windows steamed up and the smell of damp dog and gas was smothered by the smell of spicy tomato. Sitting in the van on Christmas Day, with a sleeve tugged down over a fist, they rubbed a clearing in the windscreen and watched new drops replacing old drops on the rain-bearing glass, fresh waves crashing against familiar rocks, the head of the seal holding its position in the furious sea. And they talked

about how small their life had become,   almost nothing;

about how unlikely it seemed that some society other than that of their rooms still existed,   out there.

They celebrated anyway,

contriving the sacrament of Christmas soup.

. . .

New litter, festive litter, appeared along their road in the week following Christmas.

A trickle of Quality Street wrappers that had landed, lightly, in the undergrowth as though they had flown out the driver's window of a ponderously paced car after being eaten in the same order as they had been discovered: Chocolate Finger, Toffee Penny, Orange Crème.

Later the discarded packaging of a whole, large family Christmas appeared, abandoned, in the place where the roadside stream pooled into a gully. Only the mountain saw what happened: a strange car from town with a boot-load of lumpy black sacks, a driver searching out the window for a hollow in which to stuff his cheerless gold and silver paper, his untied ribbons and unstuck rosettes.

They ate all of the Roses.

Country Fudge, Golden Barrel, Hazel Whirl, Strawberry Dream.

The final days of their eighth year were hemmed by spectacularly rising and setting suns. There was the smell of smoke from the blocks of compressed sawdust they bought in sacks from the joinery, the dogs spooning on the hearthrug. They ironed the chocolate wrappers flat between their fingers, mindlessly, and stacked them on the coffee table. They worked their way through the stack, folding each susurrant rectangle into a smaller geometric shape, scrupulously hiding the logo, reducing each to a plane of plain colour,   forming   meaningless symbols,   cellophane charms.

Voss swiftly destroyed the squeak of his ball and set to work on Pip's antler. Pip surrendered her antler and sneaked a fragment of Voss's silenced ball. She rolled it around the inside of her mouth, clacking it methodically against her tiny incisors.

Her eyes were beginning to cloud, by then, to flash blue in direct sunlight, and Voss's front legs had stiffened. After rising suddenly from the hearthrug, he would stumble for the first few steps.

The small dog had thickened with age, whereas the tall dog had shrunk. Where once one had been black and the other tan, by then
they were both
almost   completely   grey.

The Christmas socks were consigned to the bedroom sock box.

Where once there had been designated sides of the wardrobe and segregated compartments of the box of socks—the back and seat of the bedroom chair, the opposite ends of the curtain rail—this was no longer the case. By then they both selected their clothes out of the same seven-year collection of oversized charity-shop cardigans and ill-fitting jeans. They preferred grandfather shirts, woven leather belts and combinations of browns, greens and reds as opposed to blacks, blues and purples. Where once they had been tall and small, by then they were almost exactly the same height.

One had stooped, the other stretched,   and so,
from a distance, from behind, they looked
identical.

The new figurines were integrated into the Elrond shrine.

By then   the shrine dominated the living room. It formed a great mound that ascended from the timber-imitation lino to the centre of the mantelpiece. Down on the tiled dais, decorations and devotions fully encircled the stove. They planted the fawn, the pig and the Child of Prague at various stations of the mound, each facing upwards, away from the room, and toward Elrond.

They lit the fire, in December, sometimes as early as half-past four, house time. It had been over a year since they had known for sure what time it was

        outside.

Since then, the cast-iron plate in the belly of the stove had, like the glass of the door, cracked and slipped. The damaged plate interrupted the straight row of air holes at the back of the belly. In the overlong winter evenings, they sat on the Latin sofa and watched as the flames began to catch, to engulf the kindling,

    the dry moss and bark of the logs,

        the clinkers, the sawdust, the fresh blocks of coal.

They watched as the crooked air holes were illuminated, each one a black circle at the axis of an individual flame—

      an eye,   opened,

    in the very heart of their house,

             their evening.

Last thing at night,   they switched off the last light.
And the blackened house vanished into the blackened hill.
And the blackened hill vanished into the blackened mountain.
And the blackened mountain vanished into the blackened sky.

There was a blood moon
in January.

The nine o'clock news showed a picture of a huge, vivid sphere, vermillion. It will appear in the early hours of the morning, the presenter said,
high in the west and not again for another seven years.

For the first time, they experienced the house at 5 a.m., the still-
glowing stove, the subdued jungle of potted plants. For the first time
they met the night slugs, and made night tea,

and stood out in the empty yard.

The stars were lovely, but the moon was unsatisfying.

It was not vermillion, or even red. It was a smut of orange drifting
in and out of sight above the garden shed.

They drained their mugs, and went back to bed.

A wild goat came down the mountain
in January.

By January it had eaten the sedge, the rushes, the heather. It had stripped the leaves from the creeping ivy and sucked the needles off the gorse branches. Its coat was the colour of the mountain, the colour of the compacted matter between the floorboards—green, green-brown, brown, brown-green, grey—tousled and tangled like the winter-coarsened grass. Its beard dragged the mud. Its horns sailed up and out, rose and dipped and rose again in the shape of a large bird's splayed wings. Its voice was ragged and lifting. Its short tail stuck in the air when it stayed still and wagged as it trotted.

They found the wild goat on the beach.

It was champing kelp, wrack and sea spaghetti, earnestly. The shore-picking birds—wagtails, rock pipits and turnstones—scurried and tweedled in its wake.

They were interested, but not astonished. It seemed to them like the right time for the goat to descend.

It reminded them that
in eight years
still they had not
climbed the mountain.

After eight years of having lived there,
                         they finally climbed the mountain.

By then the pale patch halfway up the hedge that masked the cattle road had disintegrated. New leaves and twigs had grown and shifted to plug the old gap.

The ground webs were gone too. The spiders had died, or hiber-

nated. The shallow, handleless, dinted saucepan that sat on the concrete path had been emptied and upturned. The rucks opened by the
bullocks' hoofs across the surface of the facing field had been resealed,
healed.

The green slit in the moss-slicked skin of the living tree had sutured to
a faint scar.

    Only the stars were still all there.

                              Had they known that they would stay so long,
they would have planted a few slim, fast-growing trees: alder, willow,
silver birch.

                              Had they known that they would stay so long,
they would have re-strung the tyre swing and erected concrete blocks
in place of the withered fence.

                              Had they known that they would stay so long,
they would have nailed nest boxes to the sycamore, bat boxes to the
shingle.

                              Had they known that they would stay so long,
they would have bought a custom-designed, weather-resistant letterbox and had

                  a spare key

                          cut.

The morning that they finally climbed the mountain, from the perspective of the mouth of the path behind the farmer's parlour the sun was
not yet visible—only the colours it threw up to the cloud-belly, a blush
of champagne pink   and apricot

against the stratocumulus.

That morning, the mountain shone.

Each briar, polished by the gales, was a spear of light.

At first there seemed to be no path, and so they followed narrow part-
ings in the dead bracken, until they found, out the far side of the thickest layer of undergrowth, that there seemed to be nothing but paths.

Paths flowed across the mountain like the dry tracks of a convoluted river system,

like the petioles of a living leaf,

like the bronchi of a human lung.

Paths opened in front of them as they approached,

and closed behind them as they passed.

The needleless gorse—its height stunted by the press of the sky; its bark
scored by the scrape of the wild goat's teeth—interlaced into a waist-
high forest and clutched the ground.

Miniature eyes peered out from the black between limbs.

Miniature birds came loose from the forest.

Rock ruptured through at aberrant angles, throwing artless shadows. Boulders started to appear. Some were even-shaped or column-
like. Some were hectic-shaped but calmly balanced on lithic rostrums.
Elsewhere, smaller slabs and stones seemed to have been stacked,

shrine-like.

It was a land broken,   wasted,

positioned at the very end of time,

or perhaps,   at the very beginning,

and still in the process of being formed.

. . .

On the mountain, there was   no special weather,
   and no sign of the smudge they could see from the house.
   Up close,   it had blended in.
   Up close,   the mountain was covered with slender
feelers that probed the air, molesting the objects and creatures that
                                neared.
   On the mountain,   the mountain   appeared
                                  mountain-like,
as if, in eight years, it had accumulated stature, steadily flattened itself
upwards; as if it actually was   by then
        greater   than a hill.

From the top, they could see
   the moon and clouds; the trawlers, yachts and gannet colonies; the
towns, jeeps and chimney-pots; the turbines, trampolines, sheds and
septic tanks, the beach and the peninsula, the farmyards and slopes,
bales and slurry pits, trampolines and satellite dishes.
   From the top, they could see
   the full extension of the road they walked every day, the telegraph
poles and fence-posts in their standing ovations, the litter they knew so
well, and
                       every stray cat,
                         every cow-pat.
From the top they could see
lakes, gates, rushes, forts, floods, pubs, shrubs, tyres, bonfires.
   From the top they could see
            everything;
            all that was left.

. . .

So they counted

the standing stones, schools, and steeples:

seven,

seven,

and seven.

So they identified

their roof,

and every unpainted side of the house at once, the yellow blaze of
the lichen-encrusted gable, the weathered shed, the rusted barn, the
canopy of the sycamore, the full stretch of the lawn, the terrain over the
brow of the garden wall,   the girdling fields.

And the view from the top of the mountain,

through the uncurtained windows,

the shingle, the slates, the attic space;

through bracken, brick, wood, cement and steel

showed that   left behind in their rooms

there was but a single set of dog dishes, a single set of clothes.

One pillow,

one toothbrush,

one key,

one kitchen knife—

the traces of a sole person,   or so it seemed—

a

sole

life.

Wholehearted thanks to Rachel Parry and Cormac Boydell in whose modestly magnificent cabin I made a tentative start to this novel in the autumn of 2017; and to the Arts Council of Ireland, who awarded me a bursary in the spring of 2019 in order to finish it; and to my first and most formative readers, Deborah Baume and Doireann Ní Ghríofa; and to everyone in my publishing houses on both sides of the Atlantic, in particular Lucy Luck, Anna Stein, Lisa Coen, Sarah Davis-Goff, Pilar Garcia-Brown, and Jessica Vestuto.